Turtle in Paradise

ALSO BY JENNIFER L. HOLM

The Babymouse series (with Matthew Holm)

Boston Jane: An Adventure

Boston Jane: Wilderness Days

Boston Jane: The Claim

The Creek

Middle School Is Worse Than Meatloaf

Our Only May Amelia

Penny from Heaven

The Squish series (with Matthew Holm)

The Stink Files series (with Jonathan Hamel)

Turtle in Paradise

By Jennifer L. Holm

A Yearling Book

Text copyright © 2010 by Jennifer Holm

Cover photographs by Vstock LLC/Tetra Images/Getty Images and Eric Audras/ONOKY/Getty Images
Cover display type by Jackie Parsons

All rights reserved. Published in the United States by Yearling, an imprint of Random House Children's Books, a division of Random House, Inc., New York. Originally published in hardcover in the United States by Random House Children's Books, New York, in 2010.

Yearling and the jumping horse design are registered trademarks of Random House, Inc.

Photo credits: p. 180 (top): Little Orphan Annie © Tribune Media Services, Inc. All Rights Reserved. Reprinted with permission. p. 180 (bottom): Shirley Temple popping through 1935 calendar © Bettmann/CORBIS. p. 182: Library of Congress, Prints and Photographs Division, FSA/OWI Collection, LC-USF34-026281-P DLC (Pepe's Café). p. 183: Monroe County Library (undated postcard). p. 184: Personal collection of Cathy Porter, used by permission (photo of Kermit and family friend). p. 185: State Archives of Florida (Conch house).

Visit us on the Web! www.randomhouse.com/kids

Educators and librarians, for a variety of teaching tools, visit us at www.randomhouse.com/teachers

The Library of Congress has cataloged the hardcover edition of this work as follows:
Holm, Jennifer L.
Turtle in paradise / by Jennifer L. Holm.
    p. cm.
Summary: In 1935, when her mother gets a job housekeeping for a woman who does not like children, eleven-year-old Turtle is sent to stay with relatives she has never met in far away Key West, Florida.
ISBN 978-0-375-83688-6 (trade) — ISBN 978-0-375-93688-3 (lib. bdg.) — ISBN 978-0-375-89316-2 (ebook)
[1. Cousins—Fiction. 2. Family life—Florida—Fiction. 3. Adventure and adventurers—Fiction. 4. Key West (Fla.)—History—20th century—Fiction. 5. Depressions—1929—Fiction.] I. Title.
PZ7.H732226Tu 2010 [Fic]—dc22 2009019077

ISBN 978-0-375-83690-9 (trade pbk.)

Printed in the United States of America
20 19 18 17 16 15 14 13
First Yearling Edition 2011

For Lindsey and Shana —
the original Diaper Gang

Contents

conch

Pronunciation: 'känk, 'känch

Function: noun

1: any of various large spiral-shelled marine gastropod mollusks (as of the genus *Strombus*)

2: *often capitalized:* a native or resident of the Florida Keys

—*Merriam-Webster's Collegiate Dictionary,* 11th edition

June 1935

1

Rotten Kids

Everyone thinks children are sweet as Necco Wafers, but I've lived long enough to know the truth: kids are rotten. The only difference between grown-ups and kids is that grown-ups go to jail for murder. Kids get away with it.

I stare out the window as Mr. Edgit's Ford Model A rumbles along the road, kicking up clouds of dust. It's so hot that the backs of my legs feel like melted gum, only stickier. We've been driving for days now; it feels like eternity.

In front of us is a rusty pickup truck with a gang of dirty-looking kids in the back sandwiched between furniture—an iron bed, a rocking chair, battered pots—all tied up with little bits of fraying rope like a spiderweb. A girl my age is holding a baby that's got a pair of ladies' bloomers tied on its head to keep the sun out of its eyes. The boy sitting next to her has a gap between his two front teeth. Not that this stops him from blowing spitballs at us through a straw. We've been stuck behind this truck for the last few miles, and our windshield is covered with wadded bits of wet newspaper.

A spitball smacks the window and Mr. Edgit hammers the horn with the palm of his hand. The no-good boy just laughs and sticks out his tongue.

"There oughta be a law. No wonder this country's going to the dogs," Mr. Edgit grumbles.

Mr. Edgit ("You can call me Lyle") has a lot of opinions. He says folks in the Dust Bowl wouldn't be having so much trouble if they'd just move near some water. He says he doesn't think President Roosevelt will get us out of this Depression and that if you give someone money for not working why would they ever bother to get a job? But mostly Mr. Edgit talks about a new hair serum he's selling that's going to make him rich. It's called Hair Today, and he's a believer. He's used the product himself.

"Can you see the new hair, Turtle?" he asks, pointing at his shiny bald head.

I don't see anything. It must grow invisible hair.

Maybe Archie should start selling hair serum. If his pal Mr. Edgit's anything to go by, most men would rather have hair than be smart. Archie's a traveling salesman. He's sold everything—brushes, gadgets, Bibles, you name it. Right now he's peddling encyclopedias.

"I could sell a trap to a mouse," Archie likes to say, and it's the truth. Housewives can't resist him. I know Mama couldn't.

It was last May, one day after my tenth birthday, when I opened the door of Mrs. Grant's house and saw Archie standing there. He had dark brown eyes and thick black hair brushed back with lemon pomade.

"Well, hello there," Archie said to me, tipping his Panama hat. "Is the lady of the house at home?"

"Which lady?" I asked. "The ugly one or the pretty one?"

He laughed. "Why, ain't you a sweet little thing."

"I'm not sweet," I said. "I slugged Ronald Caruthers when he tried to throw my cat in the well, and I'd do it again."

Archie roared with laughter. "I'll bet you would! What's your name, princess?"

"Turtle," I said.

"Turtle, huh?" he mused, stroking his chin. "I can see why. Got a little *snap* to you, don't ya?"

"Who's that you're talking to, Turtle?" my mother called, coming to the door.

Archie smiled at Mama. "You must be the pretty lady."

Mama put her hand over her heart. Otherwise it would have leaped right out of her chest. She fell so hard for Archie she left a dent in the floor.

Mama's always falling in love, and the fellas she picks are like dandelions. One day they're there, bright as sunshine—charming Mama, buying me presents—and the next they're gone, scattered to the wind, leaving weeds everywhere and Mama crying.

But Mama says Archie's different, and I'm starting to think she may be right. He keeps his promises, and he hasn't disappeared yet. Even Smokey likes him, which is saying something, considering she bit the last fella Mama dated. Also, he's got big dreams, which is more than I can say for most of them.

"Mark my words, princess," Archie told me. "We'll be living on Easy Street someday."

That sounds swell to me, but even I know there's gonna be a few bumps on the way to Easy Street, and I'm sitting right next to one of them.

"You're like Little Orphan Annie and her dog," Mr. Edgit says, eyeing Smokey, who's curled up in my lap. "You know, Annie's dog. What's its name?"

How can someone have opinions on baldness and not know the name of Annie's dog? She's the most famous orphan on the radio and in the funny pages.

"You know, the dog that's always with her . . ."

I look out the window.

"The one that's always barking . . ."

"Sandy," I say.

"Right, Sandy," he says with a pleased look. "What does Sandy say, again?"

"*Arf,*" I say.

"That's good! Sandy says *arf*!" Mr. Edgit chortles. "Does your cat say *meow*?"

I roll my eyes.

"What happened to your cat, anyhow?" he asks with a sidelong glance at Smokey. "She got the mange?"

"She got burned," I say, smoothing my hand over Smokey's ragged patches of fur.

"That why you call her Smokey?"

"No," I say. "The name came first."

"I still don't understand why you couldn't stay with that old dame," Mr. Edgit says. "Place was a mansion. Looked like something Shirley Temple would live in."

Shirley Temple is this kid actress everyone's calling "America's Little Darling." She has dimpled cheeks and ringlet curls and is always breaking into song or doing a dance number at the drop of a hat. Everyone thinks she's the cutest thing ever.

I can't stand her.

Real kids aren't anything like Shirley Temple and I should know. Because Mama's the housekeeper, we get free room and board. Which wouldn't be so bad, except the rest of the house usually comes with kids. And they're *never* nice to the housekeeper's daughter.

There was twelve-year-old Sylvia Decker, who gave me her old doll and then told her mother that I stole it from her. We didn't last very long there. And then there was Josephine Stark, who told all the kids at school that it was my job to clean the toilet. No one would play with me after that.

The worst, though, were the Curley boys—Melvin and Marvin. They thought it would be funny to light poor Smokey's tail on fire and watch her run around. Mr. Curley didn't believe me when I told him what his boys did, and he fired Mama on the spot. Like I said, kids are rotten.

Mama's promised me that someday we're going to live in our own home. We've got it all picked out, too. It's a Sears mail-order house, from a kit. The Bellewood, Model #3304. This is what the brochure says:

The "Bellewood" is another happy combination of a well-laid-out floor plan with a modern attractive exterior. The design is an adaptation of a small English cottage.

There's a living room, a kitchen, a dining room, two bedrooms, and a bathroom that comes with something called a "Venetian mirrored medicine case." I don't know what it is, but it sure sounds fancy. Still, we're a long way from living in the Bellewood.

Mama says she's lucky to have a job with Mrs. Budnick considering how tough times are. I don't know how lucky I am, though. Mrs. Budnick shook her head when Mama brought our things over to her house.

"You didn't say anything about a child. Children are noisy. I can't abide noise," Mrs. Budnick said, tapping her foot.

I asked Archie if I could stay with him.

"Princess," he said, shaking his head, "I live in a

rooming house with a bunch of other men. I don't think it's exactly the kind of place a young lady should be, if you get my meaning."

So now I'm on my way to Key West to live with Mama's sister, Minerva, who I've never met. Mr. Edgit's a pal of Archie's, and since he was already going to Miami to meet with a fella about Hair Today, he offered to give me a ride. Also, he owes Archie a bunch of money. I guess Hair Today ain't exactly an overnight success.

Mama thinks me going to Key West is a swell idea.

"You'll love it, baby," Mama told me. Mama's good at looking at the sunny side of life. Her favorite song is "Life Is Just a Bowl of Cherries."

I blame Hollywood. Mama's watched so many pictures that she believes in happy endings. She's been waiting her whole life to find someone who'll sweep her off her feet and take care of her.

Me? I think life's more like that cartoon by Mr. Disney — *The Three Little Pigs*. Some big bad wolf's always trying to blow down your house.

Ahead of us, the pickup truck is swerving wildly. The kids in the back are clinging to the side.

"What's that fella doing, anyway?" Mr. Edgit asks.

"I think his tire's gone flat," I say.

A moment later, the pickup truck pulls off to the side of the road in a cloud of dust.

We slow down beside the truck. There's a worn-looking lady in the front seat staring straight ahead, a drooling toddler asleep on her lap. The fella behind the wheel is rubbing his eyes.

Mr. Edgit calls out the rolled-down window, "You need help there, buddy?"

"Do we look like we need help?" the boy in the back asks.

Mr. Edgit shakes his head. "Bunch of fools, this whole country," he says, and we start to move again.

I lean out the window, looking back. The boy blows a spitball, but we've pulled away already. It falls short, landing in the road.

2

Paradise Lost

I've never been to Easton, Pennsylvania, but according to Mr. Edgit, I'm missing out.

"Best thing about Easton?" Mr. Edgit says. "We didn't go in for Prohibition like the rest of the country. You could always get a drink in Easton."

What is it with folks always talking about where they're from? You could grow up in a muddy ditch, but if it's *your* muddy ditch, then it's gotta be the swellest muddy ditch ever.

Mama's the worst. She's always going on about how Key West is paradise—it's beautiful, the weather's perfect, there's fruit dripping from trees. To hear her talk, you'd think the roads are paved with chocolate, like something out of that dumb song Shirley Temple sings:

> *On the good ship lollipop,*
> *It's a sweet trip to a candy shop*
> *Where bonbons play*
> *On the sunny beach of Peppermint Bay.*

It turns out that getting to Key West is nearly as impossible as getting to Peppermint Bay. There's no road between some of the keys, which are little islands, so we have to wait on a ferry to take the car and us over. It's hours late because of the tide.

"This is ridiculous," Mr. Edgit grouses. "I don't owe Archie a penny more after this trip."

When we finally pull into Key West, there's not a bonbon in sight. Truth is, the place looks like a broken chair that's been left out in the sun to rot. The houses are small and narrow, lined up close together, and most of them haven't been painted in a long time. There's trash piled everywhere. It's so hot and humid it hurts to breathe.

"What a dump," Mr. Edgit says.

But it's the green peeping out everywhere that catches my eye — between the houses, in the yards and alleyways. Twining vines, strange umbrella-type trees with bright orangey-red blossoms, bushes with pink flowers, and palm trees. Like Mother Nature is trying to pretty up the place. She has a long way to go, though.

We drive around looking for Curry Lane, which is where Aunt Minnie lives, but Mr. Edgit's about as good at following directions as Hair Today is at growing hair. Finally, we park next to a little alley so that Mr. Edgit can study the hand-drawn map Mama gave him.

"I just don't understand where this Curry Lane is," Mr. Edgit says, scratching his bald head.

I wish Archie was here. He never gets lost. And he's been just about everywhere. We'll sit with a big map and he'll point out all the places he's been.

"See Chicago? Folks are smart there. And they like to look good, too. Sold a crate of hair pomade in one day," he'll say, or "That little town in North Dakota? Stingiest place I've ever been. Folks there wouldn't buy a button if their pants were falling down."

A barefoot boy with big ears is looking furtively down the alley. He's wearing overalls with no shirt underneath.

"Hey, kid," Mr. Edgit calls out the window. "Can you tell me where Curry Lane is?"

"You're looking at it," the boy says, pointing down the muddy alley.

"*That's* Curry Lane?" I ask, and the boy nods.

"Which one's the Curry place?" Mr. Edgit asks.

"They're all Currys, mister," the boy says. "It's Curry Lane."

Mr. Edgit gets out of the car and grabs my suitcase. "Come on, Turtle," he says. "At least we're in the right place."

I pick up Smokey and follow him down the lane. Mr. Edgit stops in front of a house that's so small you could probably sneeze from one side to the other. There's a boy who looks my age rocking lazily on a porch swing, his feet resting on a sleeping dog. In front of the house is a beat-up child's wooden wagon. Somebody's painted on the side of it:

WILL WURK FOR CANDY

"Excuse me, son," Mr. Edgit calls to the boy.

"What are you selling, mister?" the boy asks, flexing grimy bare feet. He's wearing one of those newspaper-boy caps set low on his forehead.

Mr. Edgit brightens. "Well, since you asked, I do happen to have some Hair Today back in my automobile."

The dog lifts its head and growls low in his throat. It's the funniest-looking dog I've ever seen, like someone crossed a dachshund with a German shepherd. It's all tiny body with a big head.

"What's it do?" the boy asks.

"Makes your hair grow," Mr. Edgit says, pointing to his head. "It's guaranteed to work in one month or your money back."

The boy snorts. "Guess *you* ain't a satisfied customer."

The dog leaps up, barking like mad. Smokey looks at him, like she can't be bothered. She's never been very scared of dogs, just kids.

"Beans! What's going on out there?" a voice shouts from inside the house.

A heartbeat later, the screen door slams open and a woman in a faded striped dress is standing in the doorway, wiping her hands on the front of her apron. She looks like an older version of Mama, except her face is tanner and her hair's pulled back in a flyaway bun.

"Hush, Termite," she orders the dog, who stops

barking with a whine. Then she turns to Mr. Edgit. "Who are you?"

"He's just some salesman, Ma," the boy says.

"I'm looking for Minerva Curry," Mr. Edgit says.

"I'm Minnie Curry," she says, her eyes widening when she sees me. "Why, if you aren't the spitting image of my sister, Sadiebelle!"

Folks have always told me that I look like Mama. My hair's brown, same as hers, but it's cut short in a bob with bangs, like a soup bowl turned upside down. Mama keeps hers long as a good dream, because that's the way Archie likes it.

Our eyes are different, though. I think the color of a person's eyes says a lot about them. Mama has soft blue eyes, and all she sees is kittens and roses. My eyes are gray as soot, and I see things for what they are. The mean boy on the porch has green eyes. Probably from all the snot in his nose.

"That's because she *is* Sadie's daughter!" Mr. Edgit says.

"I'm Turtle," I say.

"Turtle?" the boy, Beans, says. "What kind of name is that?"

"At least I'm not named after something that gives you gas," I say.

"Where's your mother?" Aunt Minnie asks, looking around.

Mr. Edgit answers for me. "In New Jersey. Where else would she be?"

"Who are you?" Aunt Minnie asks.

Mr. Edgit holds out a business card. "I'm Lyle Edgit. You can call me Lyle."

Beans hoots with laughter. "Idjit? Your name is Idjit? That's a scream, pal!"

"It's not *Idjit*, kid," Mr. Edgit says, his lips tight. "It's Edgit. Got it? *Edge-it!*"

"Whatever you say, Mr. Idjit," Beans says.

Mr. Edgit frowns at Beans and says to Aunt Minnie, "I'm a friend of Archie's."

"Who's Archie?" Aunt Minnie asks.

I'm starting to get that bad feeling I always get right before one of Mama's fellas stops coming around and breaks her heart.

"The fella Mama's dating," I say.

Aunt Minnie looks at me in confusion. "I don't understand. Why are you here without your mother?"

"Didn't you get her letter?" I ask.

"What letter? Did something happen to her?"

"Say, Mr. Idjit," Beans says loudly, "you been using that hair tonic on your arms, 'cause it's sure coming in thick there!"

It's the final straw for Mr. Edgit. He drops my bag on the porch. The dog leaps back with a startled yelp.

"I'll leave you to your happy reunion, Turtle," Mr. Edgit says with a huff, and marches down the lane to his automobile. He gets in, guns the engine, and screeches away.

"So long, Mr. Idjit!" Beans calls, laughing.

"Mama wrote you a letter," I say. "She got a new job as a housekeeper, and Mrs. Budnick doesn't like children."

"So she sent you to me?"

"I didn't have anywhere else to go."

She looks shocked. "For how long?"

"Until we can get a place of our own, I guess," I say. "Or until she gets a new job where I can live with her."

But Aunt Minnie isn't listening to me. "This is just like Sadiebelle. She never thinks. As if I don't have enough already with three kids and a husband who's never home." She looks at Smokey. "And you brought a cat?"

"Smokey's a good mouser," I say.

"She's good at being ugly, is what she is," Beans says.

From inside, a young voice calls: "Ma! I had an accident!"

Aunt Minnie closes her eyes and rubs her forehead.

"Ma!" the voice cries again.

She turns on her heel, walking through the door without a backward glance.

"Beans, help your cousin with her bag," she calls over her shoulder.

Then it's just Beans and me and the animals.

"Here," Beans says with a mean smile, picking up my suitcase. "Let me help you with your bag, *Tortoise*."

He flips it over in one smooth movement, dumping my belongings onto the wooden porch in a heap and sending my paper dolls flying everywhere. Beans walks into the house, the dog running after him, and slams the door so hard it nearly falls off its hinges.

3

Lucky as an Orphan

Folks like to feel sorry for orphans, but I think they've got it pretty good. Little Orphan Annie gets adopted by Daddy Warbucks, who's a millionaire. That's just about as lucky as it gets in my book.

I bet she doesn't have to worry about being sent to a house that's tiny and dark and smells like sour milk. Daddy Warbucks probably has a nice big plump sofa for her to sit on, and a Persian rug for her to sink her toes into. Not a wicker couch that's got a broken leg propped up with a bunch of rags and a worn braided wool rug that looks like something bad got spilled on it.

Aunt Minnie is standing in the kitchen, scrubbing a pair of soiled pants. There's a big basket in the corner, overflowing with laundry.

"Where should I put my suitcase?" I ask.

She glances at me, a harried look on her face. "The boys will have to share, I suppose. You can stay in Beans's room. Upstairs and to the left."

I climb the set of narrow wooden stairs to what looks to be more of an attic than a proper second floor. There are two rooms at the top of the landing. The door to the right one is shut. I open the one on the left and peer inside.

It's a tiny room, with an odd-looking shuttered window, like a hatch, set deep in the sloping roof. There's an iron bed and a small chest of drawers. One of the walls is covered with funny pages from newspapers—there's *Krazy Kat, Terry and the Pirates, Flash Gordon,* and even some of my favorite, *Little Orphan Annie.*

Smokey leaps out of my arms and starts sniffing at the floor. When we worked for the Talbots, our room was right next to the pantry. Mama and I would lie in bed in the dark and listen to the rats running around, searching for food. One night I woke up and there was one perched on my pillow, nibbling on my hair. I screamed so loud, Mama thought I was being murdered. After that, Mama got us Smokey, and she's slept with me ever since.

"Is that your cat?" a voice asks, and Smokey hisses. A little boy with a tuft of bright blond hair is standing there wearing a short-sleeved shirt and no underpants.

"That's Smokey," I say.

"What happened to him?"

"Some boys lit her tail on fire," I say.

"You're not from around here, are you?"

"How'd you guess?"

"You talk funny," he says, and looks down at my feet. "And you're wearing shoes."

A boy with a pair of crooked glasses walks into the room, saying, "Beans, did you take my shooter? If you fed another marble of mine to the seagulls, I'm gonna tell Ma." He stops his tirade when he sees me.

"Who're you?" he asks. He seems like he might be nine or maybe ten, but he's on the thin side, and so he looks younger.

"I'm Turtle."

"You a relation or a thief?" he asks.

"What's there to steal?" I say.

"I'm Buddy!" the little boy interjects. "You want to play marbles with me?"

Before I can answer, Aunt Minnie appears. She catches sight of the boy with the glasses and frowns.

"Kermit, you get back in bed right now, do you hear me?" Aunt Minnie says.

"But, Ma—" Kermit whines.

"Doc Parrish said you are supposed to take a nap *every day*!"

"But, Ma—"

"Do you want your heart to give out? Do you want to die? Is that what you want?"

"But I'm not tired!" he says.

"I don't care if you're tired or not! Now get in that room and go to sleep before I kill you myself!" she shouts.

Kermit marches out, saying, "I'll take a nap, but I'm still not tired."

"I don't have to take a nap anymore!" Buddy declares. "I'm four years old!"

"For Pete's sake, Buddy, go put on some pants," Aunt Minnie says in an exasperated voice. "What is the matter with you, child?"

The little boy runs out and Beans storms in, his dog right on his heels. Termite sees Smokey and starts barking. I grab my cat up and hold her out of the way.

"What's the big idea?" he says. "Why can't she stay with the little pests?"

"Beans, get Termite out of here," Aunt Minnie says.

Kermit pokes his head back in. "Beans ain't sleeping with us, Ma. No way, no how!"

"Get in bed, Kermit!" Aunt Minnie says.

Buddy comes flying back in. He's got pants on now, but it looks like they're on backward.

"Why should Termite go?" Beans argues. "He was here first! Make her ugly cat take a hike!"

"Smokey can sleep with me!" Buddy says, and snatches her out of my arms. Smokey hisses in fear, swiping at Buddy's nose.

"Ow!" the little boy cries, and drops Smokey.

The next thing I know, Termite's chasing Smokey around the tiny room, barking his head off, and Buddy's wailing about his nose, and Beans is hollering at Termite to get Smokey, and Kermit is saying there's no way he's sharing a room with Beans again, considering what happened last time, and the whole while Aunt Minnie just stands there, her mouth growing tighter and tighter like a rubber band, until finally, she snaps and hollers: "That's it! You kids get out of this house and take those animals with you before I smack every last one of you!"

And that's how I find myself sitting on the front porch with Beans, Kermit, Buddy, Smokey, and Termite.

"Don't come back inside until I say so!" Aunt Minnie shouts. She slams the door after her, muttering, "Honestly, this is what I get for kissing a Curry."

Smokey darts to safety under the house, and Termite waddles over to the lane looking forlorn.

Kermit is positively beaming at his good fortune. "Well, that's one way to get out of a nap," he says.

"Aren't you a little old for naps?" I ask.

"I had rheumatic fever, and now I've got a weak heart," Kermit says.

"Kermit almost died!" Buddy exclaims.

"Really?" I ask.

"And guess what? He said I could have all his marbles when he was dead," Buddy says, and then his face falls. "But then he went and lived."

"Sorry about that, Buddy," Kermit says.

"That's okay," Buddy says. "I'll get your marbles the next time you die!"

"Won't be too soon for me," Beans says.

A boy with black hair and bare feet comes whizzing down the lane on a battered bike. I haven't seen a pair of shoes on a single kid yet.

"Hey, Pork Chop," Beans says.

"Who's she?" the boy asks, looking at me.

"Aw, just some freeloading cousin from New Jersey," Beans says.

"Pork Chop?" I say.

Kermit shrugs. "Pork Chop and Beans. They just go together."

Across the street, a wiry-looking older man with slicked-back graying hair walks out the front door of a house not much bigger than this one.

"Well, if it ain't the Diaper Gang," the man drawls.

"Hi, Jelly!" Buddy says. "You want to play marbles with me?"

"Sorry, Buddy," Jelly says, and reaches into his back pocket to pull out a beat-up-looking letter. He holds it out to Beans. I recognize the flowery handwriting at once. It's the letter from Mama.

"Mr. Gardner delivered it to me by mistake. Been delivering mail for twenty years now and he still can't keep the Currys straight," he says. He looks at me. "Got yourself a new member, I see."

Beans thumbs at me. "You mean her? She's not in the gang. No girls allowed."

"You've got a club called the Diaper Gang?" I say. "What do you do? Change diapers?"

All the boys turn to look at me as if I'm dumb as a post.

"Course we change diapers," Beans says. "That's why we're called the Diaper Gang."

I shake my head in disbelief.

Kermit explains. "We watch babies. Bad ones."

"Bad babies?"

"The crying kind," Pork Chop says.

"You get paid?" I ask.

"In candy," Beans says.

"And we got rules," Pork Chop says with authority.

"Oooh! Oooh!" Buddy says. "I know the rules!" He squishes up his face, thinking hard. "Uh, uh, uh, uh, let me see. Number one is, it's, uh, um, I think it's, uh—"

Beans cuts him off. "First rule of the Diaper Gang is you gotta know the rules, Buddy."

"But I'm only four!" Buddy cries in frustration. "My head can't hold that many things!"

"What are the rules?" I ask.

Kermit ticks them off. "No girls allowed. Keep your rag clean. Always duck. And never tell anyone the secret formula."

"You got a secret formula?" I ask.

Kermit says, "For diaper rash."

"Cures it like *that*," Pork Chop says, snapping his fingers.

"You know how many mothers on this island want our secret formula?" Beans asks.

All three boys answer in unison: *"Every last one."*

Jelly scratches at his chin, where there's a raw red patch of skin. "You think your formula will work on this? Nicked myself shaving."

"Works on everything, Jelly," Beans says. "But it'll cost you."

"I'm good for it, Beans."

"Cash only."

"But I'm your cousin!" Jelly says.

"Who ain't on this island?" Beans says, setting his cap low over his eyes. "Sorry, Jelly. Business is business."

"You're pretty hard for an eleven-year-old, Beans," Jelly says, shaking his head.

"Gotta be hard to handle bad babies," Beans says.

"You ever take care of good babies?" I ask.

"Ain't no such thing," he declares.

Kermit grins. "That's why we're always in business."

4

The Conch Telegraph

Lots of folks go to bed hungry these days. I've heard of men fighting over scraps in garbage cans and about that lady who taught her kids to steal milk.

Because Mama works in rich folks' homes, we've had it better than most. But after looking at what Aunt Minnie sets in front of me for breakfast, I start thinking that going hungry might not be that bad after all.

I stare at my plate. There's a piece of thick toast with something green and slimy smeared on top of it.

"What is it?" I ask.

"Alligator pear on Cuban bread." Aunt Minnie purses her lips. "I don't cater to fussy children."

I pick it up and take a bite. It tastes a lot better than it looks.

"I read the letter from your mother. She says she's planning on marrying this Archie fella." Aunt Minnie raises an eyebrow. "He planning on marrying her?"

"I don't know."

"What's he do?" Aunt Minnie asks.

"He's a salesman," I say.

"Is he nice? Is he good to her?"

"He bought me these shoes."

Aunt Minnie crosses her arms. "I spent my whole childhood taking care of Sadiebelle, and here I am taking care of you now. I sure hope you have more sense than her."

I'm not sure how I feel about her saying Mama doesn't have sense, so I change the subject. "May I have a glass of milk, please?" I ask, and she says, "Help yourself."

I get a glass down off a shelf and open the icebox. A scary, insectlike creature with a pointy tail scuttles out, waving mean little claws, and I jump back. Termite starts barking but keeps his distance.

"Scorpion, Ma!" Beans says.

Aunt Minnie picks up a rolling pin from the counter and brings it down hard on the scorpion.

Kermit looks at me. "They like to hide in dark places."

"Like shoes," Aunt Minnie says pointedly, staring at my feet.

"I know," I say. "Mama warned me to shake them out before I put them on."

"She must remember the time *she* didn't shake hers out," Aunt Minnie says. She takes a dustpan and sweeps up the dead scorpion, and then walks out of the room.

"What's an alligator pear, anyhow?" I ask.

"Are all kids from New Jersey as dumb as you?" Beans asks.

"That's an alligator pear," Kermit says, pointing to a bowl of avocados.

"That's an avocado," I say. One of the rich ladies we worked for liked them in her salad.

"What does this Archie sell, anyway?" Beans asks.

"Encyclopedias," I say.

"Encyclopedias? To who?"

"Dumb kids like you, who don't know what an avocado is," I say.

The front door slams open, and Pork Chop comes walking down the hall into the kitchen.

"Ready, pal?" Pork Chop asks.

"Ready," Beans replies, smoothing back his hair and slapping his cap on. Kermit stands up.

"Can I come?" Buddy asks.

"Course you can't come, Buddy," says Beans.

Aunt Minnie walks back into the kitchen and groans at the overflowing basket of clothes in the corner. "Take Buddy with you. Turtle, too. I don't want children underfoot. I need to finish all this laundry today or Mrs. Cardillo won't pay me."

Beans frowns.

"Hot dog!" Buddy says.

Outside, the heat hits me like a slap in the face. Kermit disappears around the side of the house and returns a moment later with a load of old quilts, then piles them in the wagon.

We start walking down the sleepy lane. Kermit pulls the wagon and Buddy dawdles, stopping every few minutes to pick up stones.

"Where are we going?" I ask.

"We got Pudding today," Kermit says.

We stop by a small house that has a tree with blooming red flowers in front of it. The sound of a baby crying rings out an open window. Beans knocks on the door. It opens and I see the source of the racket: a bald, fat, red-faced baby being held by his tired mother.

"Morning, Mrs. Lowe," Beans says.

"Oh, Beans," the woman says. "I don't think I've ever been so happy to see someone!"

"How's he doing?" Beans asks.

"I swear he didn't sleep more than five minutes last night! He's teething real bad."

"Don't worry, Mrs. Lowe. We'll take care of him," Beans says.

"I just fed him," she says, and then practically tosses the crying baby into Beans's hands. She gives Pork Chop a small stack of cloth diapers and goes back inside.

Beans sticks the baby in the wagon on top of the quilts, and we start moving again. The baby's crying his head off like he's being tortured.

"What's wrong with him?" I ask.

"Nothing," Beans says. "Pudding's the worst baby we've ever had."

"It's his mother's fault," Pork Chop explains. "She spoils him. Picks him up every time he cries."

"You gotta let a baby be," Kermit says.

"That's why we don't let girls in the gang," Beans says. "Girls always want to pick up babies."

"Not me," I say. I don't like babies. They're like Shirley Temple: everyone thinks they're cute, but the fact is they're annoying. All they do is cry and make messy diapers.

Pudding is crying furiously, kicking his little feet.

"Time to wrap him up, fellas," Beans announces with authority.

If the Diaper Gang were an army, then Beans would be the general, and Pork Chop his lieutenant. Which means all the grunt work is left for poor Kermit.

"Blanket!" Pork Chop orders, and Kermit lays a thin blanket on the ground.

"Baby!" he says, and Kermit hands him Pudding.

Pork Chop proceeds to roll the baby up like a little sausage. He tucks the blanket tight around him, muffling his cries. We've barely walked a few steps when the baby abruptly stops crying, screwing his eyes shut against the sun. He's fast asleep.

"Works every time," Beans says in a satisfied voice.

"Can he breathe?" I ask.

"Ain't lost a baby yet."

"Why's he called Pudding?"

"Mrs. Lowe thought she was getting fat from

eating too much banana pudding, but it turned out it was a baby," Kermit explains.

A white-haired old man comes running down the street. He looks around and then darts down an alleyway. A moment later, a lady comes walking toward us fast. She's got a streak of flour on her cheek as if she was baking and got interrupted.

"He went that way, Mrs. Alvarez," Beans says, pointing.

"Thank you, Beans," she says in a weary voice. "Second time this morning it's happened." She smiles at me. "You must be Turtle. Nice to meet you."

"Nice to meet you, too," I say, and she walks quickly off.

Kermit taps his skull. "Old Mr. Alvarez ain't right in the head anymore. Poor Mrs. Alvarez spends her life chasing after him."

"One time he ran naked down Duval Street!" Buddy exclaims. "You should've seen it!"

"I don't think I would've wanted to see that," I say.

An iceman is making his deliveries, and Beans calls out, "You got any spare chips, Mr. Roberts?"

"Sure thing, Beans," the man says, handing out slivers of ice.

"Don't forget me!" Buddy says.

"Wouldn't dream of it, Buddy," Mr. Roberts says, giving the little boy a chip, and one to me, too. "You must be Turtle. My, I do believe you're as pretty as your mother."

I suck on the ice until all that's left is a cold memory.

"How come everyone knows who I am?" I ask.

"Conch Telegraph," Pork Chop says.

"What?"

"Conchs like to talk. Everyone knew you were here five minutes after you showed up yesterday," Kermit says. "Besides, you're related to most of them."

Mama told me that Conchs are what folks in Key West call themselves. A lot of them originally came from the Bahamas, where they fished for conch. When I asked Mama about my Conch relatives, she said her parents had been dead for a long time, but that I had a lot of Conch cousins.

Too bad she didn't tell me that they were all snotty boys.

Beans leads us to the waterfront. It's a hive of activity, bustling with boats. There's a fella selling live flopping fish right on the dock and another one who's unloading some scary-looking cargo: dead sharks.

Buddy climbs on a railing and stares down at the water.

"I sure do love watching them," he says, and I look, too.

The biggest turtle imaginable breaks the surface of the water like a lazy cow. Another pops up and then another. There's a whole crowd of them.

"What are they all doing down there?" I ask.

"It's the turtle kraals," Kermit says. "It's where they keep the sea turtles until they're butchered."

"Don't fall over!" Pork Chop says to me, snapping his teeth. "You'll end up as supper!"

"Hi, Slow Poke!" Beans calls out to a man working on the deck of a boat.

The man turns. He's tan, with sunburned patches around his neck and hair the color of caramel. He's wearing a wide straw hat.

"Hey there, Beans," he says. "I stopped in at Matecumbe and saw your dad. He said to say hi."

"Thanks," Beans says. "I hear you lost your first mate. Why don't you hire me? You know what a good sailor I am!"

"I know," Slow Poke says. "But I already hired Ollie. I'll be sure to keep you in mind for next time."

The man's cool gray eyes flick over to me and go still. "Who's your friend here?"

"That's Turtle! She's a cousin!" Buddy says. "And she's got a cat named Smokey!"

"Turtle, huh?" he says, studying me. "You wouldn't happen to be related to Sadiebelle Gifford, would you?"

"That's my mama," I say.

"Really," Slow Poke says. "Is she here with you?"

"She's in New Jersey."

"I see," he says.

"Say, Slow Poke, you get any loggerheads?" Beans asks.

"Not this time," he says. "But I did all right." He waves his thumb at the deck of the boat. It's piled high with black blobs.

"What're those?" I ask.

"That's gold you're looking at," Slow Poke says.

"They're sponges," Kermit says.

"Sure don't look like any sponge I've ever seen," I say.

"Gotta clean 'em yet. Then they'll be fine enough for a lady's face," Slow Poke says.

Pudding fusses in the wagon and Beans frowns.

"We gotta keep moving, Slow Poke, or Pudding will wake up. He's teething bad."

Slow Poke looks at the baby. "You should try a little whiskey on his gums."

"We did once," Beans says. "Didn't work."

Slow Poke winks. "Then you didn't give him enough."

5

Can You Spare
a Nickel, Pal?

Kids in the funny pages sure lead thrilling lives. Little Orphan Annie and her dog, Sandy, are always having all sorts of adventures, and then there's Terry Lee from *Terry and the Pirates*. He sails to the Far East with his pal Pat, looking for a lost gold mine.

There's nothing thrilling happening on Curry Lane as far as I can tell. And the only thing that's lost in this house is Buddy's pants. I can hear Aunt Minnie hollering at the little boy.

"Buddy," she's saying, "come on, now. Where did you put those pants?"

"I don't remember!" he says.

"Put your shirt on, at least," she says.

"I want *you* to do it for me," he whines. "My arms are too tired!"

"Too tired? You're four years old! What've you got to be tired about?"

Kermit walks in without knocking, cleaning his glasses on his shirt.

"What are you doing?" Kermit asks.

"Nothing."

"The gang's got babies today," Kermit says. "You want to come along?"

"Uh—" I start to say.

"Buddy!" Aunt Minnie yells. "You did not just have an accident!"

Kermit gives a knowing look. "You hang around here and you're gonna end up watching Buddy. Believe me, he's worse than all those babies put together."

Pork Chop and Beans already have the wagon in the lane when we step onto the porch. It's so hot I wouldn't be surprised if the hens were laying hard-boiled eggs.

"How many we got today?" Beans asks Pork Chop.

Pork Chop pulls a scrap of paper out of his back pocket.

42

"Three," Pork Chop says.

"Who said she could come?" Beans asks, looking at me.

"Just let her come already," Kermit says.

Beans shoves his hat over his eyes. "You can't change diapers, got it?"

"Fine by me," I say.

"Which means you can't get candy, neither," Pork Chop says.

In short order, the wagon is packed tight with babies, like cigars in a box. There's Pudding again, and two other babies—one named Carlos and one named Essie.

As we walk along, barefoot boys shout out to Beans.

"Hey, Beans! How're the babies today?" a grubby kid calls. "You need me, you just ask!"

"You want any help, Beans?" another one offers.

"Say, Beans, you want me to fill in until Ira gets back?"

I guess it's the same all over: everyone just wants a job.

"Where's your father?" I ask Kermit.

"He's up in Matecumbe, working on the highway," he says.

"How come you didn't go with him?"

43

"Mama didn't want to move. She said it's a wilderness up there. Poppy comes home every few weeks."

"Least he's got a job," I say.

That's the good thing about Archie. He's always had work, not like some of Mama's other fellas. Before I left home, he took me aside.

"Here, princess," he said, handing me a five-dollar bill. "For emergencies."

"Thanks," I said.

He knelt down and looked me in the eye.

"Everything's going to work out," he said. "I promise."

The wagon hits a bump, and the front-right wheel falls off, making the wagon tip. The babies wake up bawling.

"This bum wagon," Beans says.

Pork Chop picks up the loose wheel and bangs it back on.

Kermit sniffs. "I think Pudding's got a bad diaper."

"What are you waiting for, then?" Beans says.

Kermit takes the baby out of the wagon, lays him on the ground, and undoes the soiled diaper. Then he pulls a clean rag out of his pocket and wipes the bare bottom. It's red as can be.

"Look at his bungy! No wonder the kid's crying," Kermit says.

"Bungy?" I say.

"What? Kids in New Jersey don't have bungys?" Pork Chop says.

"Use the formula," Beans orders.

Pork Chop digs around in the wagon, pulls out a small cloth sack, and hands it to Kermit, who sprinkles Pudding's bottom liberally with white powder. Then he pins on a fresh diaper and plops the baby back in the wagon.

"That's the secret diaper formula?" I ask, unimpressed.

"Yep," Beans says.

"What's in it?"

Beans makes a face. "It's secret. You got to be in the Diaper Gang."

"Speaking of wanting to be in the Diaper Gang," Pork Chop says, "look who's coming."

The big-eared boy who was skulking around Curry Lane my first day comes running up to us.

"Hey, Beans!" the boy says, panting.

"Too Bad," Beans says coolly.

"I went to the lane but your ma said you'd left already," he says.

"We got babies," Beans says.

45

"See, I was wondering if I could have another try?" the boy asks, swallowing hard.

"We've given you three tries already, Too Bad," Beans says.

Too Bad starts talking fast. "But I been practicing! Honest, I have!"

Pork Chop and Beans share a look.

"Give him a baby," Beans says.

Kermit pulls baby Carlos out of the blankets and hands him to Too Bad, who looks nervous.

Beans crosses his arms in front of him. "Go on now. Let's see what you can do."

Too Bad lays the baby on the ground and unpins the diaper. He tugs a rag out of his back pocket and gives the baby a wipe. Before he can grab a fresh diaper, a stream of liquid hits him right in the face.

"Aww," Too Bad says.

Pork Chop and Beans burst out laughing.

"Rule number three," Pork Chop says, wagging his finger at Too Bad. "Always duck."

"'Specially with baby boys," Kermit adds.

Too Bad shuffles off, a disappointed look on his face.

"See ya later, Too Bad!" Beans calls.

"Yeah, too bad you'll never be in the Diaper Gang!" Pork Chop shouts.

✳ ✳ ✳

The afternoon air is steamy as a wet wool sock on a hot radiator when the Diaper Gang return the babies to their loving mothers. The boys sit on the front porch of the house on Curry Lane eating their sweet pay while I watch.

"Why don't you work for money?" I ask.

"Who'd pay us?" Beans says. "Most of the island's on relief."

"Here, you can have some of mine," Kermit says, holding out a piece of homemade papaya candy.

"Thanks," I say, but Beans snatches it right out of my hand.

"That's Diaper Gang candy," Beans says. "Don't be giving it to her."

Termite barks and Beans tosses the candy at the dog.

A bell starts ringing and Kermit exclaims, "Jimmy!"

Out on Francis Street, a throng of kids jostles around a man selling ice cream from the back of a horse-drawn wagon. Each kid takes an empty tin can and a spoon from the back of the wagon, and then waits in line.

"I want some ice cream," Beans declares.

"We ain't got no nickels," Pork Chop points out.

"Don't need nickels," Beans says, bragging. "I got charm. You watch."

Beans saunters right to the front of the line, holding out his empty can. The other kids don't seem to mind; it's like he's king.

"What flavor, Beans?" the ice cream man asks.

"Sour sop, Jimmy," Beans says, and the man deposits a scoop of ice cream in his empty can.

"That's a nickel, Beans," Jimmy says, holding out his hand.

"Can you spare me a nickel, Jimmy?" Beans asks.

"Can't do it, Beans," the man says, and takes the ice cream out of Beans's hand. "You still haven't paid me back from last time."

"But you know I'm good for it, Jimmy," Beans says, an edge of whine to his voice.

"Sorry, Beans. Business is business."

I could've told Beans that charm only gets you so far. You gotta have smarts, too. And I got smarts aplenty.

The boys slink off back to the house. I pick up a can and wait my turn in line. When I reach the front, Jimmy smiles.

"You must be the cousin from New Jersey," he says.

"I'm Turtle," I say.

"I'm Jimmy. What can I get you?"

"Do you have strawberry?" I ask.

He reels off the flavors. "I got tamarind, mango, coconut, sour sop, and sugar apple."

"I'll try the sugar apple," I say, and Jimmy puts a big scoop in my can. I'm walking away when Jimmy says, "That's a nickel, young lady."

I hold out my ice cream. "The nickel was in the bottom of the can, mister."

"In the bottom of the can, you say?" Jimmy asks skeptically.

"I'm gonna have to eat my way to it," I say. "Might take a while."

"Oh, go on," Jimmy says. "You can only get away with that once, though."

The boys are sitting glumly on the front porch when I come walking up the lane with the ice cream.

"How'd you get that?" Pork Chop asks in an unbelieving voice.

I stick my spoon in and take a bite. "Used my charm," I say.

Beans watches the ice cream drip down my chin and licks his lips.

"Say, you ain't gonna eat the whole thing by yourself, are you?" he asks.

I hold my spoon out to the side, and Smokey walks up and gives it a lick.

"Sorry. Can't share with you," I say with a smile. "After all, I'm not in the Diaper Gang."

6

The Truth of the Matter

Kids lie. We have to or we'd never get anything. But grown-ups lie, too—they just do it differently. They leave things out; they don't give you the whole story.

I'm sitting on the porch with Buddy playing with my paper dolls. They're Kewpie dolls—baby girls wearing diapers, with big wide eyes. Mama gave them to me for my last birthday.

"These were mine when I was your age," she told me.

Buddy's not very interested in the dolls.

"Don't you want to play marbles?" he asks.

Aunt Minnie pokes her head out the front door,

saying, "Buddy, don't you get to playing and forget to go—I'm tired of washing your pants," and then lets out a shriek. Smokey's so startled she leaps off the porch and runs under the house.

"Where did you get those dolls?" Aunt Minnie demands.

I hesitate and then say, "Mama gave them to me for my birthday."

"Those are my dolls!"

"She said they were hers," I say.

"Well, she must have *forgotten* about *stealing* them from me," Aunt Minnie says with emphasis.

I look down at the dolls and back up at Aunt Minnie.

"Are you sure they're the same dolls?"

"You think I don't know my own dolls?" my aunt asks, and holds out her hand.

"You want them back?"

"Of course I want them back! They're mine, aren't they?"

I pile the dolls up and hand them to her. She snatches them and gives a satisfied smile.

"Do I want my dolls back? *Pfff!*"

After she walks inside, Buddy turns to me and asks, "You want to play marbles now?"

✳ ✳ ✳

52

The next morning, I'm watching the boys run around the lane like a bunch of wild animals. They're playing a game they call klee-klee, which looks just like tag from where I'm sitting. Kermit's the fastest of them all—tearing headlong across the lane, dodging this boy and that. For a kid with a bad heart, he sure can run.

I shouldn't have been so surprised about Aunt Minnie and the paper dolls. Mama's always been a little funny with the truth. Sure, she's told me lots of things about Key West—how poinciana trees look like they're on fire when they're blooming and that the old Conch houses were built by shipwrights to sway in storms like boats—but she left out the important parts. Like about my father.

All she's ever told me is that he was a fisherman, and that he said he loved her. When she told him she was expecting his baby, she waited a whole week but he didn't ask her to marry him. A week's a long time when you're waiting on a man, I guess. Mama left Key West and hasn't been back since. My father could have three eyes or be a murderer, for all I know.

Still, I miss Mama so much I hardly know what to do. We've never been apart. I worry about her being by herself. I've been here for two weeks now, and I've only talked to her once. I called from Mrs. Lowe's house, Pudding's mother's, because Aunt Minnie doesn't have a telephone. Not that we got to say more than two words.

"It's me, Mama!" I said when she answered. "I made it!"

"Oh, baby," Mama said, and she sounded so far away. "I was so worried."

Just hearing her voice made me feel like I was wrapped in a soft blanket.

"Mama," I started to say. And then I heard Mrs. Budnick in the background.

"Sadiebelle, you know I don't allow the help to use my personal telephone."

"Sorry, ma'am," Mama murmured to Mrs. Budnick. To me she said, "I have to go, baby. I'll write you."

Mrs. Budnick could give old Mr. Scrooge a run for his money.

Aunt Minnie's voice rings through the hot air: "Ker-mit! Ker-mit!"

She's striding down the lane, Buddy stumbling to keep up with her.

Kermit freezes midstep, closing his eyes as she bears down on him.

Aunt Minnie's like a lawyer interrogating a

witness. "Look at you! All sweaty! Were you running around playing that wild game?"

"No, Ma," he says, looking down at his bare feet. "It's just the heat."

"You know Doc Parrish said you're not supposed to run around!" She turns and looks at the other boys. "Was Kermit running around?"

All the boys shake their heads, eyes wide as saucers. There's a chorus of "No, ma'am"s.

"Honest, Mrs. Curry," Pork Chop says, his voice so sincere that I almost expect a halo to pop up over his head.

"Honest? You boys are about as honest as a drunk in a tavern." She whirls on Kermit. "If I so much as catch you walking fast, I will box your ears, you hear me?"

"Yes, ma'am," Kermit says, looking chastened.

"Your heart can give out at any minute," she adds.

"Yes, ma'am."

Buddy saves Kermit from the rest of Aunt Minnie's lecture.

"Ma! Ma!" Buddy says, hopping up and down. "I gotta go! I really gotta go!"

"Oh, come on, Buddy," Aunt Minnie says, and she walks off, pulling Buddy behind her. "You better make it to the outhouse this time."

Kermit sits down next to me on the porch and groans.

"Sometimes I think it would have been better if I'd just died in the first place." He looks at me. "You want to go to Duval Street?"

"All right," I say, and we get up and start walking.

We've just turned the corner of Curry Lane when I ask, "Would your heart really give out from running around?"

"I don't know," he says with a mischievous grin. "Want to find out?"

And he takes off down the street.

Duval Street's like a different Key West. It's nicer. Kermit tells me they're trying to get tourists to come down here to vacation. There are all sorts of businesses: Gardner's Pharmacy; Einhorn's Grocery; the Plaza Restaurant; the Blue Heaven, which serves "refreshments and beer"; a big building called the Cuban Club; and a fancy hotel called the Key West Colonial Hotel. There's even a movie theater. Too bad it's playing a Shirley Temple picture.

It seems like everyone on this island has a funny nickname, because the whole time we're walking, Kermit's greeting this person and that one: "Hi, Cheap

John! Hi, Too-Too Mama! Hey, Kitty Gray! Hiya, Fat Rat, you try the doughnuts today?"

He's like the mayor, except he's nine.

We pass folks left and right who are speaking Spanish. It's the second language here because of all the Cuban folks. Even Aunt Minnie speaks it a bit.

"Say, you know anywhere I could get a job?" I ask Kermit.

"Girls ain't allowed in the Diaper Gang," he says.

"A real job," I say. "I need to make some dough."

"What for?"

"So Mama and I can buy the Bellewood," I say.

"What's the Bellewood?"

I pull out the catalog page and show it to him.

"'Monthly payments as low as thirty to forty-five dollars,'" Kermit reads, and gives a low whistle. "That sure is a lot of dough."

"Got any ideas?"

Kermit looks thoughtful. "Why don't you ask Johnny Cakes? I hear he's always looking for help."

"What kind of business does he have?"

"He's a rumrunner. He's got a fast boat!"

"He likes to run around with bottles of rum?"

Kermit gives me a funny look. "No, he *runs* it.

He brings it in from the Bahamas." He lowers his voice to a whisper. "It's illegal."

"Where can I find this Johnny Cakes fella?" I ask.

"He's probably at Pepe's."

Kermit takes me to a little café that's crowded with tables and folks sitting around drinking coffee.

"There he is," Kermit says, pointing at a handsome man wearing a smart white linen suit. There's another man at the table, a big fella with a mustache. They're drinking *leche* out of condensed-milk cans. Leche is Cuban coffee with a lot of milk. Everyone seems to drink it down here, even kids. I saw a toddler sucking down a leche a few days ago.

We walk over to the table and Kermit says, "Hi, Johnny Cakes!"

"Well, well, well. If it isn't our Kermit," the handsome man says with a broad smile. "And who's this lovely lady?"

"This is my cousin Turtle."

"Pleased to meet you, sweet cheeks," Johnny Cakes says.

"I hear you got a fast boat," I say.

"Fast enough," he says, smiling.

"You hiring?" I ask.

He looks a little uncomfortable. "I don't normally hire kids."

"I don't mind illegal activities, long as I get paid," I say.

Johnny Cakes blanches. "What is it you think I do?"

"Kermit says you're a rumrunner," I say.

"I'm not a rumrunner, sweet cheeks," Johnny Cakes says, his voice smooth. "I'm a businessman. Import-export."

Kermit looks confused. "But Cousin Dizzy said last Saturday you brought in a haul of the best rum he's ever tasted!"

"He's got you there, Johnny!" the other man says, bellowing with laughter.

"You a rumrunner, too?" I ask the man.

Kermit says, "Nah, he's just a writer."

"You write anything good?" I ask.

"What do you mean, 'good'?" the man says.

"You know, like for the funny pages." I tick off my favorites on my fingers. "I like *Little Orphan Annie*, and *Terry and the Pirates*, and *Flash Gordon*."

"Me too!" Kermit adds. "I love *Flash Gordon*!"

Slow Poke walks up and puts an envelope on the table in front of Johnny Cakes, who picks it up and slides it into his suit pocket without looking at it.

"Maybe you should start writing for the funny pages, Papa," Slow Poke says, and the writer fella grunts.

"You like the funny pages?" I ask Slow Poke.

"*Terry and the Pirates* is my favorite," he says.

"You got good taste," I say.

Johnny Cakes asks Slow Poke, "You hear about the auction?"

"Must be a war coming," Slow Poke says.

"Who's fighting?" I ask.

"That's just an old sponger saying, honey," Slow Poke says. "Sponges are used to clean wounds. So if someone's buying a lot of them, we say they're getting ready to start a war. There's a sponge auction coming up soon. I'm heading out tomorrow to catch what I can to sell at it."

"You need any help?" I ask. "'Cause this fella won't hire me to run his illegal liquor."

Johnny Cakes groans in exasperation.

Slow Poke looks at me for a long moment and then says, "I suppose I could use another hand, honey."

"All right!" I say.

Slow Poke laughs. "Meet me at the docks at

dawn. My boat's *The Lost Love*." Then he tips his hat and walks off, whistling.

"Been out fishing with Slow Poke once or twice myself," the writer fella says. "He's a first-rate sailor."

"You know, you'll never get famous unless you write for the funny pages," I tell him.

He gives me a stern look. "You in the habit of giving grown folks advice, young lady?"

"Sure," I say. "You're the ones who need it most."

7

Terry and Pat

As I walk to the docks through the gray early-morning light, I feel just like Terry Lee heading off with Pat on an adventure to the Far East. Except, of course, I'm going to be looking for sponges, not a gold mine. But I don't care; I'm excited. Also it doesn't hurt that Beans was burned up when he found out Slow Poke had hired me and not him.

"Why's he taking you if he needs another hand?" Beans asked.

"Maybe he needed a *smart* hand," I said.

Slow Poke waves when he sees me. "Hey there, honey," he says. "You ready to work?"

"You bet I am," I say.

"Waves are kicking up a little. You know how to swim, right?" he asks, helping me onto the boat.

"Like a fish," I lie.

Slow Poke gestures to another fella who's on deck. He's younger, maybe eighteen, with soft brown hair and an easy smile.

"This is Ollie. He's my new first mate," Slow Poke says.

"Welcome aboard, Miss Turtle," Ollie says, tipping his cap.

"What happened to the old first mate?" I ask.

"Got bit by a shark," Ollie says.

"That happen a lot?"

Slow Poke chuckles. "Only after a few rounds at Sloppy Joe's. The shark was a lovely lady named Margaret."

"Shark ever bite you?" I ask.

He looks away. "A long time ago."

It's a hot day, but the combination of the wind and the salt water spraying cools off my skin. Key West disappears behind us, and the ocean spreads out like a glassy blue road.

The men maneuver smoothly around the boat,

adjusting sails, tightening lines. They don't even need to talk to each other; they're like the sailing version of Fred Astaire and Ginger Rogers doing a dance number.

Slow Poke takes off his straw hat and puts it on my head. It's too big.

"What's this for?" I ask.

"Your pretty face is gonna get burned up," he says, squinting up at the sun. "It's a lot hotter than it looks."

"Mama said Key West was hot, but I didn't think it would be this hot," I say.

He looks at me sideways. "So how is your mother these days?"

"She's working as a housekeeper for a mean rich lady who hates kids and won't let her talk on the telephone," I say.

"Besides that?" he asks.

"Besides that, she's fine," I tell him. I look out at the horizon. "Say, you think we'll be attacked any time soon?"

"Attacked?"

"That's what always happens in *Terry and the Pirates*," I say.

Slow Poke nods. "I've noticed that kid gets in a lot of scrapes. But I don't think we have anything to worry about." He looks across the boat. "Ollie here will beat 'em off."

"You bet I will, Cap!" Ollie says, and holds up his fists. "Just let 'em try and get past me!"

"So where we headed, Pat?" I ask Slow Poke.

"Pat, huh?" His eyes crinkle in amusement. "I don't know. What do you think, Terry?"

"How about China?" I suggest.

"China's pretty far away. Might not be home for supper."

"I don't mind. I had a big breakfast." I look at him closely. "You ever been to China for real?"

"'Fraid not. But I've been to Cuba. And the Bahamas." He touches my nose. "Your people are from Green Turtle Key. Mine too."

"Are we related?" I ask. "Seems like everybody here is someone else's cousin."

He stares at me. "I don't know, honey."

There's something about him that tugs at me. He's so kind. And, of course, he's got good taste — he likes the funny pages.

"I wish we could go to China," I say, "just like Terry and Pat."

Ollie appears at Slow Poke's shoulder. "Pat's a lot more handsome than the cap here."

"I think I might need to get myself a new first mate," Slow Poke says, and makes a face.

"Just as long as it's not Beans," I say. "Or else you'll have a mutiny on your hands."

Ollie tosses in the anchor and Slow Poke and I climb down into a little dinghy. Slow Poke picks up a jug of some kind of liquid and pours it onto the surface of the water.

"What's that?" I ask.

"Shark oil," he says. "You spread it out on the water, and when you look through the bucket, you can see better. Helps you spot the sponges."

He picks up a glass-bottomed bucket and holds it on the water, looking down intently. Then he takes a long pine pole that has a three-pronged hook on one end and sticks it in the water, hook end first. He fishes around and then drags the pole up. Stuck on the hooked end is a black sponge.

"Good size. It's no loggerhead, but they can't all be," Slow Poke says.

I help by pointing out sponges, and Ollie and Slow Poke fish them out. After a few hours, we've got a nice pile of sponges.

"That's a good day's work," Ollie says, wiping

the sweat off his forehead and looking at Slow Poke. "What do you think, Cap?"

"I see one more," I say.

"You want to try for it, Miss Turtle?" Ollie asks, holding out the pole.

"All right," I say.

I maneuver the pole, and Slow Poke smiles at me.

"You're a born Conch," he says.

I've almost snagged the sponge when I lose my footing and go tumbling over the side of the dinghy. The next thing I know I'm underwater and I try and take a breath but I choke. All I can think is that Beans is gonna be happy that I'm dead because he'll get his room back. Then I feel a strong arm go around my waist and pull me to the surface.

"I got you, honey!" Slow Poke says, and then I'm being handed up into Ollie's arms and laid on the bottom of the dinghy.

"Spit it up, Miss Turtle!" Ollie says, and I do.

"Good girl," a dripping Slow Poke says, brushing the wet hair gently from my forehead. "Took ten years off my life!"

"She went over so fast, Cap," Ollie says, his face anxious.

"I thought you said you could swim like a fish," Slow Poke chides me.

"A dead one," I say, and cough.

"Honey," Slow Poke says, shaking his head, "dead fish float."

We're sailing for home when we pass a slip of an island with a shack. Slow Poke turns to Ollie and says, "I want to check on the cistern."

"Aye-aye, Cap!" Ollie says, and drops anchor close to the little island. The men row the dinghy to shore. I follow Slow Poke to the shack.

"Does someone live here?" I ask, peeking inside. It's tiny and smells like something died in it.

"Spongers leave their sponges here to cure sometimes. There's a cistern out back that catches rainwater that we use, too. Want to help me check on it, Terry?"

"Sure, Pat," I say.

Slow Poke lifts the lid off the big barrel, and I see a dead rat floating in the water.

"This is why we check it," he tells me.

"I hate rats," I say.

He empties out the cistern and sets it up again. Then he says, "Speaking of *Terry and the Pirates*, there's something you might like to see."

He leads me over to a big rock near the water's edge. There's an iron spike in it.

"Do you know what this is?"

"An old spike in a rock?"

His voice goes low. "It's a genuine pirate death trap. Pirates would shackle rivals to this rock and let them drown in the incoming tide. That spike held the iron shackles."

I look down at the rock and back up at Slow Poke.

"You're pulling my leg," I say.

"You got me," he says with an admiring laugh. "Not much gets past you."

"I'm smart," I say.

"But there were pirates around here a long time ago," he says.

"I don't believe you."

"It's true. See those keys?" he asks, pointing at the little islands in the distance. "There's hundreds of them. That's where pirates used to hide their ships, and their loot."

"Anyone ever find any treasure?" I ask.

"Everybody's always looking for Black Caesar's treasure. Especially after Old Ropes up and disappeared."

"Who's Black Caesar? Who's Old Ropes?

Why's everybody got such funny nicknames around here, anyway?"

Slow Poke laughs. "It's just the Key West way, *Turtle*."

"Humph," I say.

He looks out at the water. "Black Caesar was a ruthless pirate who buried his treasure here in the Keys."

"And Old Ropes?"

"An old-time sponger. People said Old Ropes spent so much time on the water that he had webbed feet."

I laugh at the image.

"One day Old Ropes came back from a sponging trip. He had a drink at the bar, and the next morning he was gone. Nobody ever heard from him again. Left his house full of furniture, food in the icebox. Even left his cat."

"How could he leave his cat?" I ask.

"Rumors started going round that he'd found one of Black Caesar's stashes and was living rich as a hog somewhere in South America. After that, everyone and their mother started crawling over this key looking for gold."

"Do you think he found treasure?" I ask him.

"I think he found trouble. Old Ropes liked

to gamble. I suspect he owed someone money and he had to get out of town fast." He looks up at the darkening sky. "Speaking of which, we better start back now, or your aunt will run me out of town."

"How'd you get the name Slow Poke, anyhow?" I ask.

"Guess you could say I've always taken my own sweet time doing things. My mother said I was late for my own birth."

"Just as long as you don't take your time paying me," I say, and I hold out my hand.

He shakes his head and digs into his pocket.

8

A Big, Happy Family

Maybe it's because it's only ever been Mama and me, but I don't understand what's so wonderful about having a big family. Someone's always fighting, or not talking to someone else, or scrounging around trying to borrow money. Far as I can tell, relations are nothing but trouble.

The Diaper Gang's got Pudding today, and Buddy, too, because Aunt Minnie has to do Mrs. Winkler's washing. She takes in laundry to make money. Kermit's right — Buddy's more trouble than a baby. He's spent the entire morning complaining. He's hot. He's tired. He's bored. He's thirsty. He needs to use the outhouse. Now he's hungry.

"I'm so hungry I can't think!" Buddy whines.

"You can't think 'cause you ain't got no brains, Buddy," Beans says.

"I got a headache 'cause I ain't got no food in my belly!" Buddy whines.

"Come on, let's go to my house," Pork Chop says.

"Mrs. Soldano makes the best *bollos* on Ashe Street," Kermit tells me. He pronounces it "BOY-ohs."

"You better not let Mami hear you say that," Pork Chop says. "She thinks she makes the best bollos in all of Key West."

A sign that says SOLDANO'S announces the little lunch counter that's set under the porch in front of a house. There's a man eating a sandwich on a stool.

"You must be Turtle!" a round-cheeked woman bustling behind the counter says with a warm smile. "I've heard a lot about you."

"All bad," Pork Chop says.

"I hope you children are hungry, because I need someone to try my latest batch of bollos," Mrs. Soldano says.

"I'm starving!" Buddy cries.

Mrs. Soldano places a plate of fried balls of dough in front of us and the boys grab them as fast as they can. I pick one up and take a bite. It's tasty, all garlicky and spicy.

"What's in them?" I ask.

"Black-eyed peas, garlic, pepper, and a few other secret things," Mrs. Soldano says.

"These sure are swell, Mrs. Soldano," Buddy says, licking his fingers. "But I think I might need to try some more to see if I like them better than the last bunch you made."

"You say that every time, Buddy," she laughs.

"Say, you win last week, Mrs. Soldano?" Kermit asks.

"I'll win this week. I picked good numbers," she says.

"Win what?" I ask.

"The *bolita*," Mrs. Soldano says.

"Cuban lottery," Pork Chop tells me.

"You'll still make us bollos when you're rich, won't you, Mrs. Soldano?" Buddy asks.

"Of course, Buddy," she says.

Mrs. Soldano makes us lunch—toasted ham and pickle sandwiches on Cuban bread and something called *flan* for dessert. The flan is delicious and creamy.

When we're done, she hands a bowl of flan to Pork Chop.

"Take this over to Nana Philly," she says.

"Mami," he complains, but she just orders, "Go," and turns to a new customer.

We walk down Francis Street, stopping in front of a house that looks abandoned. The windows have shutters that have been nailed down with boards.

"What are we doing here?" I ask.

"Bringing Nana Philly her lunch," Pork Chop says. "You think we'd come here for any other reason?"

I look at the house. "Someone lives in there?"

"You mean the shutters?" Kermit asks. "They've been up for years. She put them up for a hurricane and won't let anyone take them down. There're probably a million scorpions living behind them by now anyway."

Beans parks the wagon with the sleeping Pudding in the shade of a tree. Then the boys start to walk inside.

"You just gonna leave him?" I ask. "What if somebody takes him?"

Beans scoffs. "Who'd want him?"

"I'm not going in there," Buddy announces. "You can't make me!"

"Oh, Buddy," Beans says. "She can't hurt you now."

"I don't care," he insists, his chin jutting out. "I ain't going in!"

"Suit yourself," Beans replies, and walks in the

front door, not bothering to knock. He calls out, "Miss Bea? You here?"

No one answers back.

I follow the boys into a dark parlor. It's surprisingly cool, with little bits of light filtering in through the shuttered windows. Most of the parlor is taken up by a hulking piano that looks like it's crumbling in places.

"Termites," Kermit says, catching my look. "That piano is crawling with them. I swear this house is going to just collapse around her one of these days."

"You can hope," Pork Chop says.

"Why doesn't she just get rid of the piano?" I ask.

"Her daddy was a wrecker and he saved it from a sinking ship."

"Wrecker? You mean he's the one that broke that piano?" I ask.

"You don't know anything, do you?" Pork Chop says.

"That's Nana Philly's daddy," Kermit says, and points to an oil painting of a cranky-looking old man. Most old people are cranky. Not that I blame them. How can you be happy when you know you're gonna be dead soon?

Kermit explains, "When ships would wreck around Key West, he would salvage the cargo before it sank and then sell it off. Furniture, liquor, silk, jewelry, you name it. He was one of the richest men in Key West."

"What's Buddy so scared of?" I ask as we file down a narrow hallway.

"Her," Pork Chop whispers, looking in the door of a small bedroom.

A tiny, frail-looking old lady is sitting on a rocking chair reading a fashion magazine. She could probably use some fashion advice, considering what she's wearing: a long white cotton nightgown with a dressing gown over it, black stockings, and a red cloche hat that makes her eyes poke out like a mole peeking up at the world.

"Hi, Nana Philly," Beans says. "Miss Bea gone out?"

The old lady blinks her blue eyes fast when she sees me. She opens her mouth with obvious effort.

"Thadie," she says. It comes out in a frustrated moan.

A cheery woman with silver hair and a large straw hat bustles in and says, "Why, hello, children! I was out back hanging laundry. I didn't hear you come in."

"Hi, Miss Bea," Kermit says.

Pork Chop holds out the bowl. "Mami's flan."

"How sweet of her! Miss Philomena does love her flan," she says.

Miss Bea doesn't look much younger than the old woman in the chair.

"You must be Sadiebelle's girl! You look just like your mother." She turns to Nana Philly. "Doesn't she look just like her mother, Miss Philomena?"

Nana Philly's mouth curls up on one side, but the other side stays tugged down. It looks like she's smiling and frowning at the same time. Something about her seems familiar.

"I'm Turtle," I say.

Miss Bea smiles warmly. "We're just so pleased to meet you! Maybe you can visit sometime?"

"We gotta go, Miss Bea," Pork Chop says with a touch of impatience. "We got babies."

"Of course you do," she says. "Be sure to thank your mother for the flan, Pork Chop."

Back outside, under the glare of the hot sun, I turn to the boys.

"I don't understand," I say. "What's so scary about that old woman? She can barely talk."

Pork Chop guffaws.

"I guess you could say she was a little different before she had her accident," Kermit says.

"Nana Philly had a fit last summer and fell, and now she can't walk or talk that good," Buddy says.

"Best thing that ever happened, if you ask me," Beans says.

"You said it, pal," Pork Chop says.

"Miss Bea lives with Nana Philly now. Takes care of her," Kermit says. "Ma helps out, too, of course. Brings in lunch most days, so Miss Bea can get out for a break."

"Miss Bea's a saint," Beans says.

"You'd have to be to live with Nana Philly," Pork Chop says.

"How can you say that about a poor old lady?" I ask.

"Because she's meaner than a scorpion!" Buddy says.

"It's true," Kermit agrees.

"She said Ma would be better off dead than married to Poppy," Beans says.

"And she stood up in church and told the minister his sermon was so boring he ought to be crucified!" Pork Chop adds.

"God himself could come down from heaven, and Nana Philly would tell him he did a lousy job," Kermit says, and they all laugh.

"She hates kids most of all," Buddy exclaims. "She washed my mouth out with soap!"

"Mine too," Kermit admits.

"And mine," Pork Chop adds.

Beans nods.

"That's a lot of soap," I say.

"Old Nana Philly," Kermit says almost wistfully. "Francis Street sure is a lot quieter these days."

"How can you talk about someone's grandmother like this?" I ask.

"*Someone's* grandmother?" Beans says. "You mean *your* grandmother, don't you?"

"My grandmother? But Mama told me she was dead!"

"She's not dead. She's just mean," Kermit says.

Now I know why those eyes looked so familiar—they're the exact same shade of blue as Mama's. But why did Mama lie? And what am I supposed to do with a grandmother?

"Do I have a grandfather, too?" I ask.

"Nah, Grampy's dead," Kermit says. "Died right around the time Buddy was born."

"Wasn't my fault!" Buddy exclaims. "I was just a baby!"

"I can't believe I have a grandmother," I say.

"Believe it," Pork Chop says.

"Welcome to the family," Beans says, smirking.

9

The Diaper Gang Knows

We're splashing around in the water at the little
beach at the end of Duval Street. It's the only way to
cool off on a hot day, and every day is hot here. I
wade in up to my waist in a bathing suit that Aunt
Minnie found for me.

A beaming boy comes running up.

"It's Ira!" Kermit exclaims.

"I'm back, fellas!" the boy announces like a re-
turning hero. He's got a moplike head of curly red
hair. He looks like Little Orphan Annie without the
red dress.

"When'd you get in from Miami?" Beans asks.

"Last night. It took us forever to get home. The
ferry ran aground."

"Poppy told me that when the highway's finished we won't need no ferries," Kermit says.

"Can't be soon enough for me," Ira agrees. He strips off his shirt and dives into the water.

"What were you doing in Miami?" I ask him when he surfaces.

He gives his wet head a shake. "Who are you?"

"I'm just some cousin from New Jersey," I say before Beans can.

Ira says, "My little brother needed an operation, so we had to take him to the hospital there."

"What's he sick from?" I ask.

"Dumbness," Pork Chop says.

"Eggy lit some firecrackers and wouldn't believe me when I told him to throw them," Ira says. "He blew his thumb off, and his pinkie, too."

"How's Eggy doing?" Kermit asks.

"He's got so many of my aunts worrying over him, he can't fart without one of them jumping," Ira says. "So what'd I miss? Have we had a lot of babies?"

"The Diaper Gang was Ira's idea in the first place," Kermit tells me.

"I'm the brains of this operation," Ira says.

"I wouldn't brag about that," I say.

"We been busy," Beans says. "But we're gonna need a new wagon soon."

"Where we gonna get the dough for a new wagon?" Ira asks.

Everyone's quiet, and then Kermit wiggles his eyebrows and says, "The Shadow knows!"

The boys are always quoting the Shadow. He's a mysterious narrator from a crime radio show. I like the Shadow as much as any other kid, but you'd think if he knew so much, he'd give some advice to President Roosevelt. Far as I can tell, he needs all the help he can get.

A pretty lady with a broad-brimmed hat walks by with a handsome man.

"Pork Chop. Beans. Are you boys having a pleasant summer?" she asks.

Beans looks frozen, but Pork Chop swallows and mumbles, "Yes, Miss Sugarapple."

"See you two in the fall," she says, and they stroll off.

"Not if I'm lucky," Beans says.

"Your teacher?" I ask.

Kermit says, "Pork Chop and Beans got in big trouble with Miss Sugarapple."

"What did you do?" I ask.

"Nothing," Beans says.

"They stole the answer sheet for a test from Miss Sugarapple's desk," Kermit says.

"We didn't steal it!" Pork Chop says. "We *bor-rowed* it!"

"They had to stay after school every day for the last month and write *I will not steal* on the chalkboard two hundred times," Kermit says.

"Guess you won't steal next time," I say.

Beans sneers. "Next time we won't get caught."

After we finish swimming, we have a cut-up. A cut-up is something these Conch kids do every chance they get. Each kid brings whatever they can find lying around or hanging on a tree—sugar apple, banana, mango, pineapple, alligator pear, guava, cooked potatoes, and even raw onions. They take a big bowl, cut it all up, and season it with Old Sour, which is made from key lime juice, salt, and hot peppers. Then they pass it around with a fork and everyone takes a bite. It's the strangest fruit salad I've ever had, but it's tasty.

"Listen, fellas," Ira says, spearing a piece of potato. "I been thinking."

"About how to get us a new wagon?" Beans asks.

Ira shakes his head. "I met this kid named Lester in Miami and he told me about tick-tocking."

"What's that?" Pork Chop asks.

"All you need is a rock and string," Ira says,

lowering his voice to a conspiratorial whisper. "It goes like this."

Ira explains that you take a rock and tie it to a long length of string—long enough to reach across a roof. Then stake out a house and wait until everyone's asleep. You throw the rock over the house so that it lands on the opposite side near a window. When you tug on the string, it scrapes the window and makes a scary sound, as if a bony hand is trying to get into the house. The folks inside are scared so bad, they scream their heads off, and you take off running.

"And the best part?" Ira finishes. "No one knows who did it! What do you think, fellas?"

"I like it!" Pork Chop says. "Who should we tick-tock first?"

An evil glint appears in Beans's eyes.

"Miss Sugarapple," he says.

It's late, and I'm lying in bed, listening to mosquitoes buzz. The night air is thick with the sweet scent of frangipani. Smokey's curled into my side, her paws twitching in her sleep, like she's dreaming of chasing mice. Archie told me once that what he really sells is dreams.

"Nobody *needs* fancy face cream. A lady buys it

because she wants to feel young or find a husband or feel prettier than her neighbor," he told me. "All I do is sell her that dream, bottled up nice and tidy in a cream, or maybe a new hat, or some brushes."

"But what if she doesn't have a dream?" I asked him.

"Princess," he said, laughing, "everybody's got a dream."

I've almost fallen asleep when a scream shatters the quiet, and I know that the Diaper Gang has struck.

The Conch Telegraph kicks in the next morning.

When I go outside, the Diaper Gang boys are sitting on the porch, talking excitedly.

"That was hilarious, pal!" Pork Chop chortles. "She screamed so loud, they heard her in Cuba!"

Jelly comes walking down the lane. "You kids hear about the ghost at Miss Sugarapple's place?"

Beans feigns ignorance. "What's that, Jelly?"

"Miss Sugarapple says a ghost was trying to get into her house."

"A ghost?" Beans asks.

"Scared her nearly to death, she said."

"Gee whiz," Beans says. "I sure do hope Miss Sugarapple's okay. She's our favorite teacher."

Jelly walks into his tiny house and Beans grins. "This is the bee's knees, fellas!" he says.

Pork Chop starts laughing and says in a low, menacing voice, "Who knows what evil lurks in the hearts of men? The Diaper Gang knows!"

Pudding starts crying, and I sniff.

"I don't know about the hearts of men, but I'd bet there's something evil lurking in that diaper," I say.

Over the next few days, the Diaper Gang tick-tocks the houses of various folks who they think have wronged them, including a preacher, a store clerk who never gave out free gumballs, some man who yelled at them for picking his Spanish limes, and a girl named Lucy who sat in front of Beans in school and wouldn't let him cheat off her test.

But I guess spending all night scaring folks is starting to take its toll, because when I go down to breakfast on the third day, Beans and Kermit are practically asleep at the table.

"Late night, *Shadow*?" I ask, and Beans glares at me.

There's a knock on the door and Ira comes tromping in. He's got dark circles under his eyes, too.

"We got babies," he says, and Beans stands up

and walks out after him, Kermit and me trailing behind.

By early afternoon, everyone's drooping and not one of the boys has any patience left for the crying babies. It's just me and Beans and Ira. Kermit was only too happy to go home when Aunt Minnie hollered for him that it was time for his nap.

"I wish I had rheumatic fever so I could take a nap," Ira says.

Pudding is crying in the wagon.

Beans snaps at me. "Oh, just pick him up, why don't you?"

"I'm not in the Diaper Gang," I say.

"Who cares?" Ira says with a yawn. "We're beat."

I pick up Pudding. He nuzzles his sweaty head into the bare skin of my neck and closes his eyes, his little fist tugging on my hair. I guess this is why they warn you about picking up babies. If he stayed quiet like this, I wouldn't ever want to put him down.

Pork Chop comes limping down the lane. When he gets closer, I see that his knee's all torn up and raw-looking.

"What happened to you?" I ask him.

He spits out the words. "Too Bad."

"Too Bad followed us when we went tick-tocking last night," Ira says. "Pork Chop tripped over him."

"How could you trip over him?" I ask.

"I didn't see him! It was dark!" Pork Chop says. "I hate that kid."

"Well, you didn't have to cry so loud," Ira says, looking annoyed. "The Shadow's supposed to be mysterious! You almost got us caught!"

"You see my leg? It hurt!" Pork Chop says.

The next afternoon we're sitting around having a cut-up when Kermit comes hurtling down the lane, waving a newspaper.

"Fellas!" he exclaims. "We made the paper!"

The headline shouts *Key West Cursed by Weeping Ghost?*

"Weeping ghost?" Pork Chop says. "What are they talking about?"

"Read it," Beans orders, and Ira obliges.

" 'Is a mysterious ghost haunting the lanes of our fair town? Residents have reported strange goings-on of late. Mrs. Josephine Higgs of Peacon Lane is the most recent recipient of a ghostly visitation. "I heard her knocking at the window," Mrs. Higgs said. "I think she was trying to communicate with me." ' "

"I wasn't trying to communicate with you," Pork Chop says in an outraged voice. "I was trying to scare you!"

"Who is she, anyway?" I ask.

"My first-grade teacher," he says with a scowl.

"Boy, you sure do hold a grudge," I say.

"Keep reading," Beans says.

Ira continues: "'Mrs. Higgs believes the spirit may be the widow of a sailor who died at sea. "I never heard such a sad sound as her weeping. She was just crying her heart out. The poor thing," Mrs. Higgs said.'"

Ira finishes and looks up. Everyone is quiet. Pork Chop has turned beet red.

"Maybe you'll get your own radio show," I say to Pork Chop. "Just like *The Shadow*."

"Really?" he asks.

"Sure," I say. "You can call it *The Crybaby*."

10

The Man of the House

They say that when the stock market crashed, men were so upset at losing their fortunes that they threw themselves off buildings. I can't imagine killing myself over something like that, but then again I've never had a fortune to lose.

Pudding is dozing in the wagon under the hot sun, and Termite is chasing Smokey around the porch. Whenever Termite gets too close, my cat swipes the dog with her sharp claws. Termite howls and howls.

"Why'd you name that dog Termite?" I ask Beans.

"He followed me home one day. Ma told me to get rid of him, but no matter what I did, he always came back."

"Can't get rid of termites!" Pork Chop says.

The postman walks up. Being a postman is just about the best job a person can have. The hours are good and then, of course, there's the job security: there's no end of bad news to deliver in hard times.

"Letter for you, Miss Turtle," he says, handing me an envelope.

"Thanks," I say, and tear it open.

Dear Turtle,

How are you, baby? I miss you something awful.

Mrs. Budnick never sleeps and doesn't care if anybody else does, either. She thinks nothing of waking me up in the middle of the night to make her tea or toast. I'm so tired I can barely see straight. The only thing that keeps me going is thinking of you.

Someday this will all be behind us, I promise. I've been thinking that maybe I can become an actress. Can't you just see my name in lights? All I need to do now is get a screen test with Warner Brothers.

Love always,
Mama

P.S. Please give your aunt my love, and tell her not to kiss any Curry boys.

I sigh. This is why I worry about Mama. She's always getting zany ideas. I don't know what she'd do without me to figure things out.

"What's it say?" Kermit asks me.

"Mama's head is so high in the clouds, I'm surprised she doesn't bump into Amelia Earhart."

"How can your mama's head be up in the clouds?" Buddy asks. "Ain't it attached to her neck?"

"Look! It's Killie the Horse!" Beans says suddenly, an edge of excitement in his voice.

An old man riding a horse-drawn wagon is coming down the lane. The horse looks like it's going to drop dead any minute. I've never seen a sorrier-looking animal. And the man doesn't look much better. He's wearing filthy old clothes and has a wild, whiskery beard. The wagon is piled high with all sorts of trash.

"Murderer," Pork Chop whispers.

"What?" I ask.

"He killed a horse. Whipped it to death!" Ira says.

The man doesn't look like he could kill a fly, let alone a horse.

"Says who?" I ask.

"Says everybody!" Pork Chop says.

The boys grow quiet as the wagon passes. The next thing I know, all the boys are chasing after the wagon, taunting the old man.

Their mocking cries fill the lane: "Killie the Horse! Killie the Horse!"

They jump onto the back of the wagon.

"Leave me be!" the old man cries, but he loses his balance and goes tumbling onto the dusty lane.

The boys erupt into peals of laughter.

A lady steps out of her house and shouts, "You boys stop that right now! You hear me?"

The boys mouth a few halfhearted "Yes, ma'am"s and come sauntering back, snickering under their breath.

"You see the look in his eyes when we jumped on the wagon?" Pork Chop says. "That was swell!"

"You said it, pal!" Beans says.

Killie the Horse stands up and climbs gingerly back onto the wagon, gives a whistle, and starts off.

"What should we do now?" Ira asks.

"Maybe you should go drown some kittens," I suggest.

"Ain't no fun in drowning kittens," Beans says.

"Yeah," Pork Chop says. "You gotta light their tails on fire and watch 'em run around!"

A tall man carrying a sack over his shoulder turns onto Curry Lane and Beans inhales sharply.

"Poppy," he says, his throat thick.

Then he leaps up and runs down the lane. Beans throws himself headlong into the arms of his father, who drops his sack and hoists Beans up easily, hugging him hard. Kermit and Buddy go racing down the lane, too, shouting "Poppy's home!" Even Termite waddles to greet his master, yipping happily.

My uncle's face is tan as old shoe leather. He looks hot and tired, and has a pale patch of skin on his chin where a beard must've been.

Aunt Minnie opens the door and steps out onto the porch. She doesn't fling herself into his arms and kiss him like Mama when she sees Archie. She just wipes her hands on her apron and says, "You shaved, Vernon."

"Stopped at the barbershop on my way home," he says, rubbing his chin. He looks at me and back at Aunt Minnie, a question in his eyes. "Something you want to tell me?"

Aunt Minnie rolls her eyes. "She's Sadiebelle's girl. Just showed up."

"Got the family resemblance, all right."

"Poppy!" Buddy says, tugging on his father's hand. "Will you play marbles with me?"

Pudding, thoroughly disturbed by all the shouting, starts crying.

"That one ours, too?" Uncle Vernon asks with a jerk of his head.

"You haven't been gone *that* long," Aunt Minnie says, and everyone laughs.

Whenever Archie comes back from a sales trip, it's like Christmas. He buys perfume for Mama—Je Reviens in a tall blue glass bottle that looks like a skyscraper—and pretty things for me, like mother-of-pearl comb-and-brush sets.

Then he takes us all out for a fancy meal—chicken à la king and peach melba ice cream—and Mama dancing after.

Uncle Vernon doesn't buy treats like Archie, but things are different with him in the house. Beans is a little nicer, and Buddy has fewer accidents, and Aunt Minnie doesn't seem so tired. Uncle Vernon's got a quiet way about him. He doesn't say much at all. But I like him.

Aunt Minnie makes beef soup for dinner to celebrate Uncle Vernon being home. It's delicious. I eat three bowls.

After the dishes are done, the boys play outside in the lanes and Aunt Minnie delivers clean laundry.

It's just Uncle Vernon and me. He pulls a sewing box down off a shelf and takes it into the parlor, where he sits by a lamp. He threads a needle, picks up a shirt from a basket of clothes needing mending, and starts sewing a tear on the elbow. His stitches are small and perfect.

"Gee, I never met a man who could sew," I say.

"My daddy taught me. He was an old Conch sailor. He always said you should know how to mend your own sail." He cocks his head. "You know how to sew?"

"Sure," I say. "Housekeeper does the mending."

Uncle Vernon hands me a needle and thread and a pair of Buddy's pants. There's a tear in the bottom.

I look at the radio. "Can we listen to *Little Orphan Annie*?"

He turns it on and we sew and listen to Annie and Sandy.

"That Sandy's a smart dog," Uncle Vernon says.

"Not as smart as Smokey," I say.

"I saw that you brought a cat. What happened to her fur?"

"A bunch of mean kids did it. They tricked her with some ham and then lit her tail on fire."

"That's a hard lesson," he says. "Bet she won't let that happen again."

When I'm finished mending the tear, I hold out the pants for Uncle Vernon to see.

"Not bad," he says.

"Not much point, if you ask me," I say. "Can hardly keep pants on him."

"How are you settling in here?" Uncle Vernon asks.

"I'm not used to having cousins," I admit.

"You'll get used to them. I see you've already acquired a taste for turtle," he says.

"What?" I ask.

He looks amused. "Dinner. That was three bowls of turtle soup you had, you know."

"I thought it was beef!" I say, feeling slightly sick. "Seems mean to eat something you're named after."

"Nothing mean about filling your belly. And turtle's cheap meat." He studies me. "Where'd you get that name of yours?"

"Mama says I've got a hard shell."

And I do. I haven't cried since I was five years old. I don't think I have much of a choice, to tell the truth. Who else is going to hold things together when Mama falls apart after some man disappears? Once you get out of the habit of crying, you hardly even miss it.

"A hard shell, huh?" he says. "Must take after

your aunt. I don't know anyone who's got a harder shell than my Minerva."

"Hard as a brick," I say.

Uncle Vernon looks at me. "You know, the thing about a turtle is that it looks tough, but it's got a soft underbelly."

I don't say anything.

"So I hear your mother is seeing a salesman," he says, tying off a knot. "What's he sell?"

"Encyclopedias," I say.

"He successful?"

"Archie can sell anything," I say. And then, "Mama really likes him."

He looks at me. "What about you?"

"I like him a lot," I say. "He's not like all the others."

He nods. "You know, your aunt and your mother were the prettiest girls in Key West in their day. They couldn't walk down a lane without boys tripping in front of them."

"Mama's still pretty," I say. "Mr. Leonard swore he'd leave his wife for her."

"Mr. Leonard? Who's he?"

"Mrs. Leonard's husband," I explain. "A family we worked for."

"I see," Uncle Vernon says. "And how did that turn out?"

"Mrs. Leonard fired Mama."

"Now that doesn't seem fair."

"It wasn't. Especially since Mama was the third housekeeper Mr. Leonard proposed to," I say.

Uncle Vernon laughs. "Sounds like Mrs. Leonard should have fired Mr. Leonard."

"You said it," I say. "Good help is hard to find."

11

Ladies Who Lunch

Forget hair tonic and encyclopedias. The Diaper Gang's on to something with their diaper-rash formula.

A lady with a screaming baby appeared at the crack of dawn on the front porch.

"Is Beans home?" she asked me in an anxious voice.

"Beans!" I hollered. "You got a customer!"

Beans came to the door.

"It's Nathaniel's bungy. It's just terrible. I've tried everything. I don't know what else to do," the mother said, looking like she was going to burst into tears at any second. "Can I please have some of the diaper-rash formula?"

Beans went back inside and returned with a bag

of the formula. "But you gotta let his bungy air out first before you put it on," he advised.

"Bless you, Beans," the woman said.

A few days later, the same woman comes back. This time she's smiling, and so is the baby.

"I don't know how to thank you, Beans," she says. "The formula cleared it up right away."

"Always does."

"Here," she says, giving him a handful of tickets. "I bought one for all of you. There's a Shirley Temple picture playing."

After she leaves, I turn to Beans.

"You ought to patent that formula," I say. "You'd be the Rockefeller of diaper rash."

"I know," he says.

We're walking out the front door to go to the matinee when Aunt Minnie calls to us from where she's ironing in the parlor.

"I'm sorry," she says, wiping a hand on her forehead. "But one of you kids is going to have to go over to Nana Philly's and give her lunch. I've just got too much laundry to do today."

"Not me," Beans says quickly.

"Me neither!" says Kermit.

"No way, no how, Ma!" Buddy says.

Aunt Minnie looks up at the ceiling as if she's praying for patience. She's going to be praying a long time at this rate.

"I'll do it," I say. Nana Philly can't be any worse than Shirley Temple.

Aunt Minnie gives me a long look. "Thank you, Turtle," she says. She sounds surprised. "You're a good girl."

"Course I am," I say. "You're just used to rotten boys."

"Why, Turtle!" Miss Bea says with a confused smile when she opens the door. "How lovely to see you! But I was expecting your aunt."

"Aunt Minnie's got laundry. I'll give Nana Philly her lunch," I say.

"Aren't you a dear," she says. "Well, whatever you make her, just be sure it's soft." She lowers her voice a notch. "Her teeth aren't very good."

"All right," I say.

"I won't be long," she says, walking down the steps. "You're so sweet to do this!"

But I'm not sweet—I'm curious. It's not every day you find out you have a grandmother you didn't even know was alive. And despite what everyone says about Nana Philly being terrible, I've been wanting to see if she'll be different with me. After all, I'm a girl. Maybe she just hates boys. Wouldn't blame her if she did.

I walk into the house with fresh eyes. This is where Mama grew up. A thousand questions flash through my mind: Which bedroom did she sleep in? Did she run up and down the hallway? Did she sit at the piano? I hope not. That stool doesn't look too sturdy.

Nana Philly is sitting in the rocking chair in her bedroom reading a new magazine. She's dressed the same way as when I first saw her.

"I don't know if you remember me, but I'm Turtle," I say. "Your granddaughter."

She looks up.

"Sadiebelle's girl."

And blinks.

"Mama's in New Jersey," I explain. "She got a job as a housekeeper to a rich lady."

Nana Philly stares at me.

"I'm supposed to make you lunch. You hungry?" I ask.

The old lady doesn't say anything; she just looks back down at her magazine. It's not exactly the tearful reunion I was imagining, although maybe that blink was her way of saying she was happy to see me. Then again, maybe she has dust in her eye.

I go into the kitchen and look around. Mama's always making fancy lunches for the ladies she works for. You wouldn't even know people were standing in breadlines if you walked in and saw what they were eating: iced cantaloupe, shrimp aspic, caviar sandwiches with cream cheese, hearts of lettuce with French dressing, meringue cookies.

There's no caviar or cream cheese in sight, but there is bread on the table and milk in the icebox, so I decide to make milk toast. I toast up some bread, stick it in a bowl, and pour milk over it. It's tasty, and it's mushy.

Nana Philly eyes the bowl suspiciously when I place it on the little table in front of her.

"It's milk toast," I say. "We eat it all the time." Strange as it seems, I want her to like it.

She doesn't move and then I realize why.

"Oh, no! I forgot your spoon," I say, and rush back into the kitchen. I hear a thump, and when I return, the bowl is lying facedown on the floor, milk splattered everywhere.

"What happened?" I ask.

Nana Philly doesn't say anything. Not that I really expect her to.

"I must have put it too close to the edge," I say, and clean up the mess. Then I set about making another bowl of milk toast. I bring it out—with a spoon this time—and place it in front of her on the little table.

"Here you go," I say. "I hope you like it."

She looks at the bowl for a moment and then her hand whips out and knocks it right off the table and onto the floor.

I'm so shocked, I just stand there. I didn't really believe what the boys said about her before, but I do now.

"You did that on purpose," I say. "Why? I'm your granddaughter!"

Her mouth twitches as if this amuses her.

Something hopeful in me hardens. She reminds me of all the rotten kids I've ever lived with.

"You don't scare me," I say.

I clean up the mess again and make another bowl of milk toast. But this time I don't give it to the mean old lady who's my grandmother; instead, I sit down in a chair and start eating. She stares at me, her eyes following every spoonful.

"This is delicious," I say, and smile. "Shame you spilled yours."

I swear I can see her mouth watering.

When Miss Bea returns, Nana Philly and I are sitting in the parlor.

"Did you two have a nice lunch?"

"We had a lovely time," I say.

"Would you like to come again tomorrow? Give your poor aunt a break?" Miss Bea asks.

"Sure," I say, and smile sweetly at Nana Philly. "I'm looking forward to getting to know my grandmother."

Miss Bea's waiting for me on the front porch with her shopping basket when I arrive the next afternoon.

"There's grits-and-grunts-and-gravy on the stove and guava duff for dessert. There's plenty for both of you," Miss Bea says. "I've got shopping to do, so I might be a while."

"Take your time," I say.

"Thank you, Turtle," she says. "You're a dear."

Nana Philly's in her room looking at her magazine as usual. I notice it's upside down.

"Must be some real interesting reading you got there," I say.

The old woman ignores me, so I go into the kitchen. I spoon out two bowls of grits-and-grunts-and-gravy. Folks here eat this all the time. Grunts are little fish and grits are like porridge. That's the one good thing about Key West: there's food everywhere — hanging from trees, in the ocean — and it's all free.

After what happened yesterday at lunch, I figured Nana Philly would have wised up. But I guess you can't teach a mean old lady new tricks, because the bowl hasn't been in front of her for more than a moment when her hand knocks it off the table. It falls to the floor in a splatter.

"You know, there sure are a lot of hungry folks who would have liked to eat that," I say, but all she does is stare at the upside-down magazine a little harder.

I clean up the mess and eat my own lunch with her watching the whole time. It's uncomfortable, but it's just like dealing with a rotten kid: if you back down in front of them, they'll never leave you be.

When I'm finished, I carry a bowl of guava duff out and place it in front of her. She lifts her hand to smack it, but I snatch it away just in time.

"You're not wasting dessert," I say. "*I'll* eat it."

I sit down and take a bite. It's delicious. It tastes a little like plum pudding.

"Miss Bea sure is a good cook."

Nana Philly pretends to ignore me, but I can tell she's watching. She reminds me of a lobster, with her beady eyes peeking out at me from under her red hat.

"Mama's a good cook, too. She makes the best caramel custard. One of our old employers, Mr. Hearn, couldn't get enough of it. He had her make it four nights a week."

I study Nana Philly closely. "You know, Mama told me you were dead."

She glances down quickly, and it comes to me.

"You were mean to her, too, weren't you?" I ask. "Is that why she hasn't come back to Key West?"

My grandmother doesn't look up, and I know the answer to my own question.

"Poor Mama," I whisper. Chased off by her own mother. No wonder she's such a wreck.

A shadow crosses Nana Philly's face and, for a brief moment, I see something like regret in her blue eyes, but then it's gone.

✳ ✳ ✳

It happens just like in the Bible: on the third day, there's a miracle.

"I can tell the old girl's really looking forward to seeing you today," Miss Bea says.

I doubt that, but say, "Really?"

"Even had me get out her best hat," Miss Bea says.

I'm not impressed. I didn't even want to come here today after what I learned yesterday, but Aunt Minnie got used to me helping out, so I don't have any choice now. This is what I get for being a good girl.

When I walk into the bedroom, Nana Philly puts down her magazine and looks at me. She's wearing a royal blue hat with a peacock feather.

"You expecting the queen?" I ask.

Miss Bea has made conch chowder, and it's simmering on the stove. I fill two bowls and carry them out, placing one in front of Nana Philly. I sit down with my bowl and start eating, waiting to hear her bowl hit the floor. But when I look up, she's holding the spoon. She brings it to her mouth with her good hand and swallows the chowder.

She takes another spoonful. And another.

Soon her bowl is empty.

"You know," I say, "I missed seeing a matinee the first day when I came here to give you lunch. It was a Shirley Temple picture."

Her eyes fly to my face.

"Which is fine by me, because I hate Shirley Temple," I say.

A corner of my grandmother's mouth turns up in a crooked smile, and her eyes shine.

"Me thoo," she says.

12

Hard Times

Everyone's always saying that hard times bring out the best in people, but far as I can tell, the only thing that hard times bring out is plain meanness. I left my shoes outside on the front porch last night, and some rotten kid stole them.

I loved those shoes. I remember the day Archie bought them for me. He'd taken Mama and me out to lunch at the counter at Woolworth's. After, Mama was buying me a pair of glue-on soles to help stretch my too-small shoes when Archie stopped her.

"The princess needs new shoes," he said. "That's all there is to it."

He took me to a store where a pal of his worked and bought me a pretty new pair of Mary Janes.

Even though Mama's fellas were always buying me treats—candy, hair ribbons—the shoes felt different. They were so ordinary, like something that, well, a *father* would buy. Walking down the street in those new shoes with Archie and Mama, it almost felt like we were a real family.

It's August now, and everything's hotter. It rains most days, quick afternoon showers that turn Curry Lane into a bowl of mud. Uncle Vernon's gone back to Matecumbe, and he took a little bit of Aunt Minnie's good humor with him.

We're on the porch as usual. Smokey's asleep in a patch of sun, and it's so hot that Termite can't be bothered to chase her. He lies under the swing, panting in the thick heat.

A bunch of kids come riding down the lane on their bikes. I eye their feet for my stolen shoes, but none of them are even wearing any.

"Who do you think took my shoes?" I ask.

"I wouldn't put it past Too Bad," Pork Chop says. "That kid's got it in for us since we won't let him be in the gang."

"Do we have to watch babies today?" Buddy asks.

"We have to watch you every day, Buddy," Beans says.

Aunt Minnie walks out and drops a basket of laundry in front of me. Termite yelps, startled.

"Your cat made a mess in my clean laundry," she says through gritted teeth.

Everyone looks at me, and I look at the laundry.

Sure enough, some cat has done something despicable on a lady's pale blue silk slip.

"Smokey would never do that," I say. "She knows better."

"She's the only cat in the house," Aunt Minnie says. "That slip's ruined. I'm gonna have to pay Mrs. Felton for that. I'll be lucky if I don't end up owing her more than she owes me."

"I swear it wasn't Smokey," I say. "Maybe it was Buddy."

"It wasn't me, Ma!" Buddy says. "I only go in my pants!"

My aunt takes a deep breath and looks down at the laundry and then back up at me.

"If it happens again, the cat's going," she says.

Then she picks up the laundry basket and marches back into the house.

Smokey blinks a sleepy eye open.

* * *

A few days later I'm walking down Grinnell Street, my toes squishing in the mud. I'm tempted to use the money Archie gave me to buy some shoes, but I don't think this is the kind of emergency he meant.

There's a bar where the sailors and fishermen like to waste their hard-earned money. Slow Poke's sitting outside at a little table with another fella.

"Well, if it ain't my favorite deckhand," he says.

"Hi, Pat," I say.

"Hi, Terry," he says.

"So when we going to China?" I ask.

"Whenever you want," he says.

"Sooner the better. I sure could stand to find that gold mine," I say. "Some kid stole my shoes."

"What do you need shoes for, anyhow, Conch kid like you?" Slow Poke teases.

"To walk in," I say.

The man sitting across from Slow Poke says, "Just like her mother, ain't she?"

"Believe me, I'm nothing like Mama," I say.

Slow Poke stares at me. "You do have a little bit of Sadiebelle in you. She wanted to see the world, too."

"How well did you know my mama, anyway?"

I ask. The other man at the table starts choking, like his drink went down the wrong pipe.

Before Slow Poke can answer, Kermit races up to me, Buddy hot on his heels.

"Ma's burning mad!" Kermit says. "She just about blew her top!"

"Smokey ruined Mrs. Felton's skirt! She's in trouble now!" Buddy says, and my heart sinks.

When I reach the house, Aunt Minnie is waiting for me on the front porch, holding out the skirt.

"Please, Aunt Minnie," I say, "I just know it wasn't Smokey. She's never done that before and we've lived in a lot of different places. Some other cat must have gotten into the house!"

She doesn't say a word; she just shakes her head.

The supper dishes are washed and the house is quiet. I'm in my room, trying to figure out what to do with Smokey. If I were Little Orphan Annie, Daddy War-bucks would rescue me and Smokey. But I'm not lucky as an orphan.

"What are we gonna do, Smokey?" I say, rubbing her belly as she stretches on the bed. We've never been apart. Having to give her up is almost worse than being sent away from Mama.

Kermit walks in without knocking, Buddy right behind him. The little boy's got his pajama shirt on backward, but at least he's got pants on for a change.

"Poor Smokey," Kermit says.

"I'm gonna miss you!" Buddy says, and lunges for Smokey, but my cat's too fast. She leaps out of the way.

"I'm not gonna miss your ugly cat," Beans says, standing in the doorway.

"Who are you gonna give her to?" Kermit asks.

"You should give her to Pork Chop," Beans suggests.

"I don't think so," I say. "I've seen him with babies."

A piercing scream rings through the tiny house.

"What was that?" Kermit asks.

"Sounded like Ma. Do you think someone's tick-tocking us?" Beans asks.

There's another scream and we all rush downstairs.

I don't think I'll ever get the picture out of my head: Aunt Minnie in her cotton nightgown, spinning wildly in circles, smacking her back, and screaming, "Get it off me! Get it off me!"

Buddy is frozen, staring at his mother.

"Get it off me!" Aunt Minnie screams.

"Get *what* off you, Ma?" Beans asks. "I don't see anything!"

Kermit turns to me, a fearful expression on his face. "Is Ma going crazy like old Mr. Alvarez? Is she gonna start running naked down Duval Street?"

Aunt Minnie lifts her nightgown over her head and throws it on the ground, clawing at her bare back.

"She *is* going crazy!" Kermit says in dismay. "She is going crazy!"

But before Aunt Minnie can make it to the doorway, let alone Duval Street, she faints dead away, falling face-first on the wooden floor.

"Aunt Minnie!" I cry.

Smokey, who's followed us down, runs into the room, hissing at the abandoned nightgown. A huge scorpion, much bigger than the one in the icebox, runs out, tail waving.

Beans yelps, jumping back. "She's not going crazy, you dummy! She got stung!" he says, then yells, "Buddy! Watch out!"

Buddy blinks as if waking up, and jumps out of the path of the scorpion.

Smokey isn't scared, though. She starts batting the scorpion around with her paws like it's a mouse.

"Be careful, Smokey!" I shout.

"I'll get the rolling pin!" Beans says.

By the time he returns, Smokey's already done the job: the scorpion's not moving. But neither is Aunt Minnie.

"Mama's dead!" Buddy wails, and starts bawling.

I rush over to Aunt Minnie's side and hear her moan softly.

"She's not dead," I say. "But one of you better go fetch a doctor!"

Kermit races out of the room.

"I don't want Ma to die!" Buddy cries. Liquid trickles down his leg and he starts crying even harder.

"Oh, Buddy," Beans says, and puts his arm around his brother.

Across the room, Smokey bites the head off the scorpion and chews.

Aunt Minnie is lying in bed on her stomach, a sheet draped lightly over her. The doctor gave her an injection.

"I've never seen anything like it. She was stung clear down her back," he says. "The scorpion was in the nightgown?"

"Must've been hiding in there," Beans says.

"She's going to be in a lot of pain. Vomiting. Just keep her comfortable. Where's your father?"

"He's up in Matecumbe," Beans says. He looks as pale as his mother.

"Well, if anything changes, you know where to find me," the doctor tells us. "I'll be by again in the morning to check on her."

We pile pillows on the floor next to Aunt Minnie's bed and stay by her side through the night. Sometime toward dawn, I wake up and go out to use the outhouse. When I return to the room, Aunt Minnie's awake. Her eyes are glazed with pain.

"Sadiebelle?" she whimpers.

"It's me, Turtle, Aunt Minnie," I say. "You got stung by a scorpion."

"I've missed you, Sadiebelle," she says.

"I'm back now," I say, and pat her hand. "Go to sleep. I'll take care of you."

Her eyes flutter shut.

"Sadiebelle," she whispers.

"Yes?" I say.

"Why'd you take my dolls?"

"Oh, go to sleep already," I say, and she does.

It's late in the day when Aunt Minnie staggers out to the kitchen, wincing with every step. She looks around, her sharp eyes taking in everything. The boys are sitting around the table, eating their supper.

"What are you children eating?"

"Milk toast," I say.

"Who cleaned?" she asks, her voice hoarse.

"Me," I say. If there's one thing a housekeeper's kid can do, it's clean.

"Buddy, have you had any accidents today?" she asks.

"I made him stop playing and use the outhouse," Beans says. "He whined every time, but I made him do it."

"You take your nap, Kermit?" she asks.

"A whole hour, Ma," Kermit says.

She stares at us all and shakes her head as if she can't believe it. Then she turns, walking slowly out of the kitchen.

Buddy pipes up. "Smokey killed the scorpion that bit you, Ma! Bit its head right off!"

Aunt Minnie pauses, and for a moment, I think she's going to change her mind. But then her eyes rest on the laundry in the corner and her shoulders stiffen.

"The cat's still going," she says.

13

Believing in Monsters

In my opinion, the fellas who make Hollywood pictures are really just salesmen. Instead of peddling girdles, they sell thrills and chills, and folks eat them up. Not me, though. I'm no sucker. I know there's no such thing as giant apes climbing skyscrapers or mummies walking out of tombs. But just try telling that to the boys.

"Who do you think would win in a fight, Dracula or Frankenstein?" Ira asks, popping a piece of alligator pear into his mouth. We're on the porch having a cut-up.

"Dracula. He'd suck Frankenstein's blood out," Kermit says.

"Frankenstein's already dead. He ain't got no blood," Beans says.

"Yeah, but he's got brains," Pork Chop says.

"Too bad you don't," I say.

Aunt Minnie opens the door and hands me a covered dish.

"Here's her lunch," she says.

When I walk up to Nana Philly's front porch, Smokey is waiting for me on the steps.

"Glad to see me?" I ask my cat. Miss Bea was only too happy to take in Smokey when I told her the situation.

I miss having Smokey with me, but I think Termite misses her even more. I can tell by the way he circles the house looking for her. The wag's gone out of his tail.

"Miss Philomena has taken a real shine to that cat of yours," Miss Bea says, opening the door.

"They've got a lot in common," I say. "They both hate kids."

Nana Philly and I have our lunch—grits-and-grunts-and-gravy, and fresh sugar apples for dessert. She hasn't knocked any food on the floor since that last time, unless you count what she gives to Smokey. Miss Bea's right—Nana Philly's crazy about my cat. She feeds Smokey the best bits from her plate and lets her sleep on her pillow, curled up around her head.

I'm not sure, but I think my grandmother might like me a little, too, even though I am a kid. She really listens to me when I talk, which is more than I can say for most grown-ups. I tell Nana Philly about the families we've worked for, like crazy Mrs. Stark, who would only let Mama buy Waldorf toilet tissue because she was convinced other toilet tissues had arsenic in them, and Mr. Barry, who kept pretending to go to work every day for two months, even though he'd lost his job. Sometimes I catch Nana Philly looking at me, and she seems sad, and I wonder if she's thinking about my mother. I know I am.

We finish our lunch and then I help Nana Philly into her bed, where she takes a nap. I'm in the kitchen washing up when I hear a loud crash. I run into the parlor thinking it's Nana Philly. But it's not my grandmother who's making the racket: it's my cat. Smokey's fallen through the top of the crumbling, termite-eaten piano and she can't get out. I hear her meowing pitifully inside, her paws scrambling.

"Hang on," I tell her.

I push the bench over and climb up and pull her out. She leaps out of my arms and runs off.

"That'll teach you to not jump on furniture."

There's a hole in the top of the piano and I look inside, curious. It's a mess—all bits of decaying wood and termite wings—but something catches my eye: a cigar box. It must have been in the piano for a long time, because there's a thick layer of dust on it. I open it.

Right on top is a pile of little shells, and beneath that is a folded-up piece of paper, and beneath that is a gold coin.

I hold the coin in my hand, turning it over. Then I unfold the paper. It's some kind of a map. I read the words at the top.

This being Where Blacke Caesar putte His Treaffure

I stare at it for a long time, but I don't believe for a moment that it's real. That'd be like believing in bloodsucking vampires and mad scientists bringing dead men to life.

I close the cigar box, put it back inside the piano, and pretend I never saw it all.

But it's funny. Even though I try to forget the coin and the map, I can't stop myself; I go back and look at them every chance I get. I keep thinking that maybe they are real. It's like monsters. You know there's no such thing, but you can't help but wonder if they're out there somewhere in the dark night, just waiting to get you.

Finally, I can't take it anymore. I go looking for Slow Poke. He'll know if the map's real or not, and I trust him. But when I get to the docks, his boat's gone.

"Sorry, Turtle. He left this morning," Ollie says.

"How come you didn't go with him?"

Ollie looks sheepish. "He's doing an errand for Johnny Cakes. Didn't need any extra help."

"Know when he'll be back?" I ask, and he shakes his head.

When I return to Curry Lane, the Diaper Gang's playing marbles.

"Fellas," Ira says, "we're not working Labor Day. Even the Diaper Gang deserves a day off!"

"You said it, pal," Pork Chop says. "Besides, I hear there's a circus coming to town!"

"Do you think there'll be elephants?" Buddy asks.

"If we're lucky, there'll be a tiger and it will eat you," Beans says. "And you better put some pants on before Ma comes home and beats your bungy good."

. "Too late," Kermit says.

Aunt Minnie's walking down the lane, and she looks mad.

"Your father won't be coming home this weekend after all!" she says. "He picked up some extra work helping out a fella on his house up there."

Nobody says anything, and she sighs.

"At least he's getting paid," she says, and then looks at Buddy. "Buddy, where are your pants?"

"I can't find 'em," he whines.

"Honestly," she says, and grabs him up and carries him into the house, his wiry body wiggling the whole way.

Beans turns to the boys, rolling a marble between his fingers. "Come on, fellas. Let's go challenge those White Street boys to a game."

As they start to walk away, I squeeze the coin in my pocket. I picture Mama on her hands and knees scrubbing Mrs. Budnick's floor and I make a decision.

"Wait a minute," I say.

Pork Chop says, "No girls allowed."

"I think this is a lot more interesting than a marble game," I say, and hold out the gold coin.

"Where'd you get that?" Beans asks.

"Nana Philly's house. It was in the piano."

"The piano? What was it doing in there?" Kermit asks.

"I don't know. But this was with it," I say. I pull the map from the pocket of my dress and hand it to Ira.

He looks at it, his eyes widening in disbelief. "It's a map! To Black Caesar's treasure!"

Hearing Ira say it out loud makes it seem real, and for a moment, I can almost see the treasure glinting under the sun—shiny gold and silver coins and jewels big as coconuts. I have to dig my nails into the palm of my hand to stop from trying to reach out and grab it.

"Don't be a sap. It's fake," Pork Chop says, but there's something in his voice, as if he's trying to talk himself out of it.

Kermit is holding the gold coin. "Looks pretty real to me. Nana Philly's daddy was a wrecker. Who knows what he took off ships!"

"Give it here," Beans says, snatching the map from Ira. He studies it. "This is the sponger's key, with the cistern and the shack."

"How do you know?" I ask.

He looks down his nose at me. "Because I been sailing since I was in diapers."

"Fellas, fellas!" Ira says, his voice humming with excitement. "What if it is real? Just like with Old Ropes? This could be big! Bigger than King Kong!"

The boys turn to Beans, waiting for his judgment, and I find myself holding my breath along with them. Is this how all those men on Wall Street lost their fortunes? Did they follow a dream so big they couldn't see that they were chasing fool's gold?

Beans gives a reluctant nod and says, "All right."

"When do we go?" Ira asks, and then they're all talking at the same time, about shovels and boats, and I can't help but think that this is exactly like something a Hollywood screenwriter would tap out at his typewriter. And I just bet some dumb director would cast Shirley Temple to play me.

14

Lying, Stealing, No-Good Kids

It's a fact: if a kid is being nice, he's probably up to no good. I guarantee you some kid was behind the *Titanic* sinking. He probably offered to steer the ship so the captain could get a cup of tea.

We tell Aunt Minnie what Pork Chop and Ira are telling their mothers, that we're gonna wake up early and go fishing for conch so that they can make conch stew for Labor Day.

"That's nice," Aunt Minnie says. "Too bad your father won't be here to enjoy it."

Ira is waiting for us on the porch when we walk out into the dark. The sun's not even up yet. He's got a roll of maps in one hand, a shovel in the other, and a canteen slung on his shoulder. The lane is empty, except for a black cat with a streak of white fur down its back, skulking around. It looks like a skunk.

"Where's Pork Chop?" I ask. He's been in charge of getting us a boat.

"Here he comes," Beans says.

Pork Chop's running down the street, huffing and puffing. He's carrying a bulging sack.

"What's that?" I ask.

"Mami was worried we'd be hungry. She made us breakfast and lunch and some snacks, too."

We walk quickly through the quiet streets. The only person we pass is Killie the Horse driving his sorry wagon. At the docks, boats bob in the water.

"Which one's ours?" I ask Pork Chop.

"Right here," he says, stopping in front of a boat with a motor. He hops in, and the boys pile in after him.

"Sure is nice," I say.

"And fast!" Kermit adds.

"Rumrunner needs a fast boat," Ira agrees.

"Wait a minute," I say. "Whose boat is this?"

"Johnny Cakes's," Pork Chop says.

"Johnny Cakes is letting us use his boat?"

Pork Chop shrugs. "Not exactly. But he'll never know. He's in Cuba."

"We're *stealing* Johnny Cakes's boat?" I exclaim.

"We ain't stealing it," Beans clarifies. "We're *borrowing* it."

The sun is high and hot. Everyone has caps on except me, and I can feel my cheeks baking. I should have listened to Slow Poke about wearing a hat. In fact, I probably should have just waited until he got back, because if Slow Poke and Ollie were Fred Astaire and Ginger Rogers, then Pork Chop and Beans are Laurel and Hardy, with Ira and Kermit thrown in as a couple of stooges.

They bang around the boat, tripping over each other and arguing about which way to go and who gets to be captain. We circle the same key again and again and seem to be completely lost. At this rate, we really might end up in China.

Finally, the little key with the shack is in sight. I can hardly believe it. We sail as close as we can and then Beans hollers, "Throw in the hook, Pork Chop!" Everyone leaps into the shallows with their shovels and wades to shore. Ira unfolds the map and looks around.

"We just need to find this tree," he says, tapping the paper. "It looks like a *Y*."

I look into the thick jungle and remember something Archie told me.

"I hate selling in the country," he said. "Trees fall. Roads get washed out. Nature changes things. Sometimes you can hardly recognize a place you were at a year before."

"How old do you think this map is?" I ask.

Ira studies it. "Pretty old, I guess."

"Then the trees are all gonna be different," I say. "Might not even be around anymore."

Pork Chop doesn't care. He grabs up a shovel and walks into the thick brush.

"Follow me," he says. "I got a nose for treasure."

By late afternoon, we're hot, dirty, and exhausted. We've dug a dozen holes all over the key, and all we've found is a whole lot of nothing. It's like looking for hair on Mr. Edgit's head.

Pork Chop flings his shovel at a tree with a growl of frustration.

"You got a nose for dirt," I say.

"I think I'll buy some ice cream with my share of the treasure," Kermit says, nibbling on a bollo.

Pork Chop grunts. "Your share? All you've done is eat."

"I got a weak heart," Kermit says.

"But not a weak stomach," Beans observes. "You better not eat all those bollos."

"Maybe we're just looking in the wrong spot," Ira says, wiping a filthy hand across his forehead.

Beans is staring at the ground, a scowl on his face. "There is no right spot."

We all look at him.

"That map's not real." He shakes a finger. "I think mean old Nana Philly put it there knowing we'd find it."

"But, Beans," Ira says, "that doesn't make any sense. If she knew about the map, don't you think she would have mentioned it to somebody a long time ago? Nobody can keep a secret in Key West!"

"You know she hates kids," Beans counters.

"Yeah," Pork Chop says in quick agreement. "That'd be just like her."

"We been had, fellas," Beans says, and points at me. "Should've known better than to listen to a girl."

"This is why we don't let girls in the Diaper Gang in the first place," Pork Chop says.

Ira looks at me, disappointment clear in his eyes. But Beans is not to be denied.

"Let's go, Pork Chop," Beans says. "Maybe we'll make it back in time to get some ice cream."

"You said it, pal," Pork Chop says, and they start walking away. "I say we try that nickel-on-the-bottom trick."

Ira and Kermit linger with me. They don't want to give up the dream, either.

"They're right," I say. I must have been crazy to believe in something like pirate treasure.

Ira sighs.

"Come on," I say. "We better go, or they'll leave us here."

I've only taken a few steps when my foot catches on something and I go tumbling backward, my bottom hitting the ground hard.

"Ow!" I cry, and look down at the culprit: a thick stone, the size of Buddy's head.

"You okay, Turtle?" Ira asks.

Pork Chop looks back at me on the ground and starts laughing. "Look! She fell on her bungy!"

Beans joins in, hooting with laughter, and a moment later I start laughing, too. I can't help it! Because it *is* funny. It's the funniest thing ever. I laugh and laugh and laugh.

Pork Chop and Beans stop laughing and look at each other like they think I've gone loony.

"You think the sun's getting to her?" Pork Chop asks.

I'm still laughing. "My bungy found it!" I say. "My bungy found it!"

"What's she talking about?" Beans asks, walking back.

"That," Ira says, staring at the stone I tripped over. It has a letter carved in it.

C

"So what?" Pork Chop says. "It's a *U*."

"Have you ever even *been* to school?" I ask. "It's a *C*."

Beans sucks in his breath.

"For Black Caesar," Ira whispers.

15

A Dream Come True

Maybe Mama is right after all. Maybe life is like a Hollywood picture, with happy endings around every corner. The boy gets the girl. The millionaire adopts the orphan. The poor kid finds the pirate treasure.

"Hot dog, that's a swell lot of gold," Kermit says.

"You can say that again," I say.

"Hot dog, that's a swell lot of gold!" he shouts with a grin.

It took longer than we thought to dig up the rotting trunk. What was left of it, anyhow. It was buried deep beneath the stone.

Now we're all just standing around, staring at the pile of dirty gold coins. You'd think when a dream comes true you'd scream until your heart gives out, but the reality is you just turn dumb from the wonder of it all.

"What do we do now?" Ira asks.

"Whatever we want, pal!" Beans hoots. "We're rich! Rich!"

And then it's like a dam cracks and we're yelling at the top of our lungs, hollering so loud a bird goes shrieking out of the trees like a newsboy on a corner.

This is how Little Orphan Annie must have felt after Daddy Warbucks took her in: she's never going to have to worry about anything ever again! She's the luckiest orphan in the entire world!

"This is better than winning bolita!" Pork Chop crows.

"How much you think it's worth?" I ask.

"Millions!" Pork Chop says. "We're rich as Rockefeller!"

Beans looks up at the sky. "We better get a move on, fellas. It'll be getting dark soon."

We empty out what's left of the food from Pork Chop's sack and pile the gold in.

"I gotta go," I say. "I'll meet you at the boat."

I do my business, and when I reach the shore the boys are standing there staring at the horizon. It takes me a moment to figure out what they're looking at — or *not* looking at.

"Where's the boat?" I ask.

"Halfway to Cuba, probably." Beans's expression turns thunderous. "Pork Chop here never threw in the hook!"

"I threw it in," Pork Chop insists. "I did!"

"Then what happened to the boat?" Beans asks.

"I—I—I don't know!" Pork Chop stammers. "Maybe someone just came along and took it!"

I can't believe it. I knew I should have waited for Slow Poke.

Ira holds up his hands. "Fellas! It'll be okay. There's always boats coming past here. Every sponger uses this key. Someone will pick us up. We'll be fine."

"How fine are we gonna be when Johnny Cakes finds out we lost his boat?" I ask.

Kermit turns pale.

"We'll buy him a new boat," Ira says. "We'll buy him a hundred boats! We're rich!"

Kermit cracks a smile. "Oh, yeah. I forgot."

There's plenty of water to drink in the cistern, but that's the only good news. All that's left to eat is three bollos and half a Cuban sandwich, which we divvy up.

"None for you," Beans tells Kermit. "You already ate more than your share."

We pile inside the small shack to sleep, lying on the ground next to each other. It's worse than being forced to watch a Shirley Temple picture. At least a theater is air-conditioned, which is more than I can say for the shack. But that's not even the worst of it.

The place is buzzing with mosquitoes.

"They're gonna eat us alive," Kermit says, smacking his arm.

The boys jostle each other for room.

"Get your elbow out of my face!" Beans snaps.

"It's not in your face," Pork Chop says.

I lie on the filthy floor and try to ignore the pests—insect and boy—by telling myself that it's just one night. There are folks all over the country who've lost their homes—they're living in tents, in boxcars, under bridges. I can survive one night in a shack.

"Stop touching me!" Beans says.

"I'm not!" Pork Chop says.

"This is all your fault anyway," Beans growls. "If you'd just set the hook . . ."

"I did!" Pork Chop shouts.

"You didn't!" Beans shouts back.

Pork Chop leaps up. "I don't have to take this from you! I'm leaving!"

"No, you ain't! I'm leaving first," Beans says, and he rushes past Pork Chop into the night.

Then it's just me, Ira, and Kermit.

"Well, at least there's more room now," Ira says with a sigh.

"Yeah," Kermit agrees. "And it'll be quieter, too. Beans snores. I haven't had a good night's sleep since Turtle got here."

I smack a mosquito. "You ain't gonna get a good one tonight. I can't believe we're stuck here."

"We'll get picked up in the morning. Don't worry," Ira says in a reassuring voice. "Just think about how we're going to spend all this gold."

The bag of treasure is under his head like a pillow.

"Guess we can afford a new wagon for the gang," Kermit says.

"We can even get two!" Ira pipes in.

"And all the ice cream we can eat!" Kermit says. "You think I can buy myself a new heart?"

"Sure," I say. "Be sure to give your old one to Beans. He could use one."

"What about you, Turtle?" Ira asks. "What are you gonna buy?"

I don't even have to think it over.

"New shoes," I say.

"Shoes?" Ira laughs. "Nobody wears shoes around here."

"Who said I was planning to stick around?"

I squeeze my eyes shut. I dream I'm walking into the Bellewood in pretty new shoes—through the front door, under the arch, and into the living room, where Mama and Smokey are waiting for me. It's so real I can smell Mama's perfume.

"I told you we'd have a happy ending," she says with a smile.

Then a mosquito bites me and I wake up in the pitch-dark shack with Ira's stinky feet in my face and Kermit drooling on my neck. Talk about a good dream turning into a nightmare.

16

The Rescue Party

If this was a Hollywood picture, the rescuers would show up at dawn with the sun, the audience would clap, and that would be The End.

When I walk out of the shack in the morning, the only thing that's shown up is muddy-looking clouds that hang low in the sky. It's drizzling and we're all scratching at our mosquito bites. My face feels hot and tight. I wonder what Shirley Temple would do in this situation. Probably sing a song about how fun it is to be stuck on an island.

"Say, you got any of that diaper-rash formula on you?" I ask Ira.

"Why didn't I think of that in the first place?" he

says, and digs in his pocket. He takes some and then tosses the bag to me.

I smear the powder on the bites and on my sunburned face, too. It helps a little.

My stomach rumbles. "I'm hungry."

"What if we don't find anything to eat?" Kermit asks.

"Then we'll starve to death," Pork Chop snaps.

The two boys returned to the shack some time during the night. They're both acting like cranky babies now. Even Pudding is easier to take than these two.

We spread out, foraging. When we meet back up, we toss what we've found into a pile: two empty cans, a rotting coconut, and a crab that's been dead awhile, judging from the smell.

"Can't even make a cut-up out of this," Ira says in disgust.

"Maybe we could build a raft?" Pork Chop suggests.

"With what?" Beans asks.

"Wood from the shack," Pork Chop says.

"Then we won't have anywhere to sleep!" Kermit protests.

"Who cares about sleeping? Let's just try and get out of here!"

"We wouldn't even be here in the first place if you weren't such a dummy," Beans says under his breath.

"I got more sense in my bungy than you've got in your whole body!" Pork Chop shouts back.

"Sense? Even Buddy knows how to set a hook," Beans says.

"I'll show you a hook!" Pork Chop growls, and clocks Beans on the side of the head with a huge roundhouse swing. I practically see stars myself as Beans goes down.

But he doesn't stay down long. He comes up roaring and rushes Pork Chop, landing on top of him as Pork Chop's head barely misses a rock.

"Come on, fellas," Ira says. "Knock it off!"

The boys roll back and forth on the ground, kicking and grunting and throwing wild punches at each other.

What is it with boys and fighting? I'm amazed any of them get to be grown-ups the way they're always going at it.

I turn to Ira. "If they kill each other, I get their share of the treasure."

Pork Chop has Beans half-pinned against the ground, with one arm wrapped around Beans's neck.

Beans's face is turning bright red when Kermit dives into the mess.

"Get off my brother!" he shouts, and leaps on Pork Chop, and then the three of them are rolling around.

Of course, Ira has to get in on the action, too, although I'm not sure whose side he's on. I just sit there and watch them. Finally, I can't take it anymore.

"Hey, look!" I call out. "A boat!"

The boys stop fighting instantly.

"Where?" Pork Chop asks. It looks like someone got in a good punch to his right eye. "Where?"

"It was there just a minute ago," I say.

Beans wipes a trickle of blood from his nose and gives me a dark look. "There's no boat! You lied to make us stop fighting."

"You got me," I say, looking skyward. "I don't know *what* I was thinking."

Pork Chop and Beans aren't speaking to each other. They sit on opposite sides of the shore, brooding. They're acting like sweethearts who had a falling-out.

"They should just kiss and make up already." I look at Kermit. "They ever scrap this bad before?"

He shakes his head. "They've been best pals since they were in diapers."

It rains on and off as we watch for passing ships. The waves are kicking up, foam frothing. Ira, Kermit, and I take turns playing checkers using gold coins and shells.

"I'm starving," Kermit says.

I know how he feels. I've never been this hungry before. Now I know why people go crazy, because all I can think about is food. I picture the fancy ladies' lunches Mama would make: cheese soufflé, potato salad, buttered nut bread, and her famous caramel custard.

"When we get back, the first thing I'm gonna eat is ice cream," Kermit says.

"What flavor?" I ask.

He doesn't hesitate. "Sugar apple."

"Me too," I say, and I can practically taste it. "You think anyone's looking for us?"

"Probably the whole town by now," Ira says.

Kermit frowns. "I'm not sure I want to be found. Ma's gonna tan our bungys good. We're not going to be able to sit for a week."

"Hey, Ira. Anyone ever tell you that you look like Little Orphan Annie?" I ask him.

"I got eyes in my head. She's just got circles," he says, looking past me at the horizon.

"You see a boat?"

"Those low clouds. And the sea foam."

"What about them?"

"Any Conch kid knows what they mean."

"Haven't you figured out I'm not from around here?"

"A storm," Ira says. "A big one."

The sky grows dark, and the wind picks up. The rain begins to fall harder, so we take shelter in the shack. Well, those of us who have sense, anyway. Pork Chop and Beans won't come into the shack because they don't want to be near each other.

Raindrops pelt the flimsy shack like spitballs. The storm is scarier than anything I've ever been in before. I keep waiting for the shack to blow away— and us with it.

"I guess Nana Philly wasn't as dumb as everyone thought, keeping those shutters up in case of a storm," Kermit says.

"She's got more sense than Pork Chop and Beans," I say.

"They're just stubborn," Ira says.

"They're just dumb," I say.

I can't stop thinking about Ira's brother, Eggy. Dumb kids get hurt. And these are two of the dumbest boys I've ever met in my entire life.

"I don't want to spend all this pirate gold buying a headstone," I say.

"I'm not going out there!" Kermit says. "I got a weak heart."

"I'll go," Ira offers.

Before Ira can even stand up, the door slams open and Beans is standing there, sopping wet.

"Beans!" Kermit says.

Beans doesn't say anything; he just pulls the door shut behind him and sits down on the ground.

Water sprays through cracks in the walls and drips in from gaps in the roof. Nearby, a tree snaps.

"Your hand sure is gonna be sore," I tell Beans.

"From what?"

"From writing *My best friend died in a storm because I was so stubborn* two hundred times."

"Shut up," Beans growls.

"Pork Chop's still out in that," I say.

"Serves him right," Beans says.

"He could be dying."

"He ain't."

"How do you know?"

Beans sighs loudly. "Because I passed him on the way in. He's standing right outside the shack."

I open the door and look out into the darkness. Sure enough, Pork Chop is huddled next to the shack.

"You coming in or what?" I ask.

He pushes past me into the shack without a word.

Inside, Pork Chop and Beans sit as far away from each other as they can. But this doesn't last very long because a big wave rushes in and we're forced to stand up and scoot back until we're pressed tight against the wobbly wall. I guess it's a good thing I'm not wearing shoes, because they'd be soaking wet.

"You think the water's gonna come up any farther?" Ira asks, his voice shaking.

I feel something long and slimy slide over my ankle and go still. I look down to see what seems like a worm disappearing into the shadows. Only I know it isn't a worm—because worms don't have whiskers or little feet.

"There's a rat in here," I hiss.

"Rat?" Kermit bleats. "Rat?"

"It's looking to stay high and dry, pal," Beans says.

"They're gonna eat us alive!" Kermit whimpers, and then he shrieks. "One just ran over my foot!"

There's a horrible cracking sound as a piece of the roof is torn away.

"We're all gonna die," Pork Chop says in a dull voice.

"Aw, come on, pal," Beans says awkwardly, but Pork Chop's too far gone.

"We are! And it's all my fault because I didn't throw in the hook!" And then he starts to cry softly.

Pork Chop's tears break the boys faster than any fistfight. They all start bawling.

Something washes over me and this time it's not water: it's *fear*. What good is all this gold if we're dead? What if I never see Mama again? She doesn't even know I'm stranded on a key with a bunch of dumb boys. I would give a million bucks just to see her blue eyes and hear her voice one last time. To hug her tight and tell her how much I love her.

The boys are crying, and I feel the fear rising in my throat like a dark tide. I try to push it down, but it bubbles up, it's swamping me, and I do the only thing I can think of. I start singing that stupid Shirley Temple song.

> *On the good ship lollipop,*
> *It's a sweet trip to a candy shop*
> *Where bonbons play*
> *On the sunny beach of Peppermint Bay.*

After a few moments, Beans's high, squeaky voice joins mine, and then Ira starts singing, Kermit too, and finally Pork Chop. We sing our hearts out. We're so good we should be in pictures; we should get a screen test with Warner Brothers. I can see our names in lights already.

The wind howls, but the Diaper Gang of Key West belts out a song as the angry storm washes everything away.

17

A Hollywood Ending

Little Orphan Annie and Terry Lee get into scrapes, but they always get rescued. Everything ends up okay in the end. But it turns out that real life's not like the funny pages.

When morning comes, no one's knocking down the door looking for us. It's still raining on and off, and windy.

Trees have been blown over and the ocean water is cloudy, the bottom churned up from the storm. There's debris everywhere and the key looks smaller, as if it's been swallowed up by the ocean.

We sit in the shack, our stomachs growling. We're past talking; there's nothing to say. We all know it: nobody's going to find us. We're done for.

The brash, cocky members of the Diaper Gang are gone, and in their place are scared kids who dream of being in their mothers' arms. Kermit's the worst, though. The boy who hates naps just sleeps and sleeps.

Night falls again and this time it's almost a relief. I think it's easier for the boys to cry in the dark. But I'm dry-eyed; crying wouldn't even touch the feeling inside me. We press into each other for comfort, no complaining now. Sometime during those long hours, Beans reaches for my hand without a word, and I fall asleep with his fingers curled in mine.

I dream that I'm sitting next to Shirley Temple. She isn't as cute in person as she is on the screen. And she's definitely wearing too much lipstick.

A hush falls over the room as the man onstage announces the next category.

"And for being the only girl stranded on an island with a bunch of boys with no chance of rescue, this year's award goes to . . ."

He opens the envelope and smiles.

"Turtle!" he says.

The audience explodes into applause.

I turn to Shirley Temple. "Sorry, Shirley. Maybe next year."

As I make my way to the podium, flashbulbs go off, blinding me. I blink awake.

Light's streaming in through the holes on the roof and I'm lying on top of the Diaper Gang, like they're a pile of puppies, an elbow digging in my belly.

A voice hollers, "Turtle! Kids!"

The door crashes open and Ollie's standing there, breathing hard.

"Cap!" he shouts. "I found 'em!"

Slow Poke shoulders past Ollie, relief spreading across his face, his eyes fixing on me.

"Honey!" he says, swooping me up in his arms. I bury my face in his warm, solid chest and I know everything's going to be okay.

The boys leap up around me.

Slow Poke holds me out so he can look at me. "Oh, honey. Your poor face."

"What took you so long, Pat?" I ask.

He makes a strangled noise. "We been looking for you kids since your aunt raised the alarm. But we had to put in once the hurricane started blowing."

"That was a hurricane?" I ask.

"It sure was, Miss Turtle," Ollie says.

"What about home?" Pork Chop asks.

"Key West came through it all right," Ollie

says, and hesitates. "But word is, the Upper Keys got hit hard."

Kermit blanches. "Poppy!"

Slow Poke pats him on the head. "He's fine, Kermit. He wasn't even there when it hit. He came back when he heard you kids went missing. You probably saved his life."

We walk out of the shack and see a motorboat in the water. A man is standing on shore, chewing on a cigar.

"I seem to be missing a boat," Johnny Cakes says.

"We're in for it now, fellas," Ira says under his breath.

The rumrunner walks over to us, slips off his fine white linen jacket, and wraps it around my shoulders. He tips my chin up. "You look like you could use a leche, sweet cheeks."

"It wasn't us, Johnny Cakes!" Beans says.

"That's interesting," Johnny Cakes says. "Because Killie saw you taking it."

"You'd believe a horse killer over us?" Beans blusters.

"I'd believe an honest man over you," Johnny Cakes says.

Beans bites his lip.

I look over at Slow Poke. "How'd you figure out we came here?"

"That kid who's always tagging around after you," he says.

"You mean Too Bad?" Pork Chop asks.

Ollie nods. "He heard you talking about digging up treasure on this key."

"We were saved by Killie and Too Bad?" Pork Chop smacks his head. "Aw, we're never gonna live this down, fellas."

Slow Poke scolds us. "Your mothers have all been worried sick. What were you kids thinking?"

"We were thinking about *this*," Beans says, and thrusts out the sack. The gold coins spill out.

Slow Poke's jaw drops so far, I'm surprised it doesn't hit the ground.

"I don't believe it, Cap!" Ollie says.

"And we're not sharing one thin dime with you," Pork Chop says with a trace of his old self.

Johnny Cakes puts a hand on Pork Chop's shoulder and squeezes. "We'll see about that."

It seems like everybody and their cousin is waiting for us at the docks. Even Nana Philly is there, sitting in the back of a wagon. She smiles when she sees me, although Beans swears I imagined it.

"Smiled at a kid?" he says.

The best sight turns out to be Uncle Vernon, wearing a scruffy beard. The news coming in from up north is terrible: they're saying lots of folks are dead from the hurricane, many of them the men who'd been working on the overseas highway. But not Uncle Vernon. It's probably the only time in history a bunch of lying, stealing, no-good kids actually saved someone's life.

The hurricane makes headlines, but so do we.

We're eating ice cream on the front porch. We're Jimmy's best customers now.

Kermit is running down Curry Lane, waving a newspaper.

"We made the front page!" he shouts.

GANG OF CHARMING KIDS FINDS PIRATE TREASURE LOOT WORTH $20,000!

"Charming?" I say to Beans. "Guess they never met you."

"Why'd they say 'Gang'?" Ira asks. "It's *Diaper Gang*. Two words."

"My eyes are closed! Why'd they print that photo?" Kermit asks.

"Better than with your eyes open," Beans says.

Not everyone's happy about our good fortune, though.

"It ain't fair! I would've gotten all your marbles if you'd died," Buddy complains.

"Sorry about that, Buddy," Kermit says.

Jelly walks out his front door.

"Well, if it ain't the Diaper Gang," he says. "That a new wagon?"

"It sure is, Jelly!" Ira says, stepping back to reveal a brand-new wagon. The boys don't have to work for candy now that they're rich, but they do anyway. Beans claims the babies need them.

We'd been back in Key West for a few days when an antiques-dealer fella appeared and paid twenty thousand dollars cash on the spot for the treasure. After Johnny Cakes was paid back for his lost boat, the rest of the money was split up six ways between me, Kermit, Beans, Pork Chop, Ira, and Nana Philly. After all, it was her map, even if she didn't know about it in the first place. She's already bought a new hat, and Miss Bea says she wants to get the piano fixed.

My money's waiting for me in the bank. Well, except what I used to buy a new pair of shoes.

Strange as it sounds, I'm having a hard time getting used to wearing them. They're pretty as a postcard, but they pinch my toes and my feet are hot and sweaty.

"Got a new member in your little gang, I see," Jelly says, looking at Too Bad, who's straightening up the blankets in the wagon.

Too Bad beams from ear to ear. "That's right! I'm in the Diaper Gang now! I saved their lives!"

Pork Chop groans, as if the idea still pains him.

"And guess what?" Too Bad exclaims. "I know the secret formula! It's cornstarch!"

"Too Bad!" Pork Chop hollers. "First new rule of the Diaper Gang is 'Shut up, already!'"

Too Bad winces. "Sorry!"

"Cornstarch?" I echo. "Your secret diaper-rash formula is cornstarch?"

"Nobody would believe us if we told them," Kermit says.

Aunt Minnie comes walking down the lane.

"I didn't have an accident, Ma," Buddy says quickly, although he's squeezing his legs together.

"The day's young, Buddy," she says, and looks at me. "Turtle, can you come inside for a moment, please?"

I can't tell if Aunt Minnie's still mad at me or not. When we got back to Key West after the storm, her eyes were red like she'd been crying for a long time. She gave me a quick hug and then shook me — shook me so hard that my teeth rattled in my head.

"Don't you ever scare me like that again! You're the one who's supposed to have some sense!" she said.

I go into the kitchen and she tucks a strand of hair behind her ear.

"I just came from Mrs. Lowe's," she says. "Your mother called. She's in Miami. She'll be here as soon as she can get a boat in."

My heart leaps. "I would've gotten stranded on an island a whole lot sooner if I'd known that would make her come get me!"

My aunt purses her lips. "Your cat can come back here if you'd like."

"Really?"

She looks embarrassed. "You were right. It wasn't Smokey. When you children were on that key, another cat snuck in here and made a mess."

"The cat happen to look like a skunk?" I ask.

She pauses and then says, "I should have believed you."

"I know," I say, and she laughs.

"I'm not sure Nana Philly's gonna want to give Smokey back," I say. "She's sweet on her."

"Maybe we can trade Buddy for Smokey," Aunt Minnie says, and grins wryly. "At least until he's toilet-trained."

I'm at Pepe's, drinking a leche with Johnny Cakes and the writer fella, recounting our adventure.

"What happened next?" the writer fella asks me, smoothing his mustache.

I lean forward. "That's when the rats showed up, Mr. Hemingway."

His eyes bulge out. "Rats?"

"Hundreds of them! They were crawling all over us. Worst thing you ever saw!"

Slow Poke strolls up. "Hundreds of rats, you say? Strange how that didn't make it into any of the newspaper accounts," he muses.

"Writers never get the story right," I say.

Slow Poke laughs and pops a wide-brimmed hat on my head. "Keep your pretty face from getting burned."

Kermit runs up to our table.

"Turtle! Turtle!" he says.

"What's the big hurry, Kermit?" Johnny Cakes asks.

Kermit starts coughing.

"Easy there, son," Slow Poke says, handing him a leche.

Kermit gulps the coffee and then looks at me. "Turtle! Your mother's here!"

"Sadiebelle's here?" Slow Poke says.

"She's at the house!"

Curry Lane has never seemed longer than when I'm running down it toward Mama. My hat flies off, but I can't be bothered to stop; nothing's going to keep me from my mother.

"Turtle!" Mama cries.

She rushes down the steps of the porch, and then I'm in her arms, and I'm home again.

"Oh, baby," she says, and stands back, looking me up and down. "Just look at you! You're so tan."

"I missed you, Mama," I say.

A deep voice says, "Miss me, too, princess?" and Archie's walking out the front door, wearing his Panama hat.

"Archie!" I cry, and run to him. He picks me up and twirls me around, putting his Panama hat on my head.

"You can call me Daddy now," he says.

"You got married?" I gasp.

I look back at Mama, and she waves her hand at me, a thin gold ring glinting in the sun. She's smiling so wide she's practically glowing.

"Oh, Mama!" I say, and I feel her happiness like my own. It's as if a weight has lifted off my heart, and for the first time in my life I can breathe.

Archie sets me down, looking serious. "Nothing like a tragedy to make you realize what's important. Soon as your mother told me what happened, we started driving."

Beans, who's sitting on the porch swing, says, "Say, how's your pal Mr. Idjit doing, anyhow? His hair grow in yet?"

Slow Poke is loping down the lane. His eyes light up when he sees Mama.

"Sadiebelle," Slow Poke says, and smiles. "It's been a long time."

"Slow Poke," Mama says, going still.

"Mama," I say, tugging on her arm. "Slow Poke's the one that rescued us."

"He is?" she asks.

Archie wraps an arm around my shoulder and looks at Slow Poke. "In that case, I owe you a debt, sir, for looking after our little girl here."

Slow Poke's smile slips.

"This is Archie," Mama says. "My husband."

"You're married?" Slow Poke asks.

"Newlyweds," Archie says, and sticks his hand out to Slow Poke. "Archie Meeks. Pleased to meet you."

Slow Poke doesn't shake his hand.

"Huh," Slow Poke says in a hollow voice, "too late again." And then he turns and walks quickly down the lane.

"What a funny fella," Archie says with a laugh. "And what kind of name is Slow Poke?"

I look up at Mama. "What did he mean, 'again'?"

"Nothing, I'm sure," she says, and smiles a little too brightly. Then she links her arm in mine and says, "Come on, baby. I'm dying to show Archie Duval Street."

It's like the happy ending of a Hollywood picture: Archie and Mama and me strolling arm in arm along Duval Street, a perfect family.

"On the way down here, we passed a nice piece of land in Georgia," Archie says to me.

"Georgia?" I say.

"Good lot. Peach trees. A little brook."

"The perfect place for the Bellewood," Mama finishes.

"Took the words right out of my mouth," he says.

"What about Mrs. Budnick?" I ask.

"I quit," Mama announces with a laugh. "No more scrubbing floors for me!"

"We'll be hiring the help from now on, thank you very much," Archie says.

"Long as we're nice to the housekeeper's kid," I say.

Archie looks down at me from under his Panama hat. "I told you we'd be here someday, princess."

"Duval Street?" I ask.

He smiles. "Easy Street."

18

Paradise Found

Something's been bothering me about Little Orphan Annie. After she was adopted by Daddy Warbucks and went to live in his mansion, did she ever miss the orphanage? Late at night, when she was lying in her soft new bed, did she ever think about the orphans she left behind?

I'm starting to feel like Little Orphan Annie. I've got my very own fancy room next to Mama and Archie's in the Key West Colonial Hotel on Duval Street. The sheets are crisp, and the pillows are plump. It's probably the nicest bed I've ever slept in. But that's just the problem: I can't sleep. I keep thinking about Aunt Minnie and Uncle Vernon and Nana

Philly and Miss Bea and the Diaper Gang and Slow Poke and Johnny Cakes and Mrs. Soldano, and even Too Bad, who turned out not to be so bad after all. Seems to me like he should get a new nickname.

At breakfast, Archie asks, "You ladies all packed?"

"Yes, indeed," Mama says.

"Aren't we gonna say good-bye to Aunt Minnie and Uncle Vernon?" I ask Mama.

"Of course," she says.

Archie nods in agreement. "I'll check out of the hotel and arrange to get the luggage over to the docks. I'll meet you at your sister's place at noon. That should leave plenty of time to say your good-byes and for us to make our boat."

"That sounds perfect," Mama says. "Don't forget to stop at the bank, Mr. Meeks."

He tips his hat. "As if I would forget, Mrs. Meeks," he says, and she giggles.

After he's gone, Mama turns to me and gives herself a little shake.

"Isn't this like a dream come true?" she asks. "I feel like Cinderella!"

"She scrubbed floors, too," I say, and swallow. "Mama, can I ask you something?"

"Of course, baby," she says.

"How well did you know Slow Poke?"

Her smile doesn't falter, but her voice trembles a little.

"Not very well at all, as it turned out," she says, and that's when I know.

I know that my father doesn't have three eyes and isn't a murderer, unless you count sponges. He's kind. And he likes the funny pages.

Just like his daughter.

"Enough about that," Mama says briskly, and stands up. "We better hurry along and say good-bye to Minnie. I wish we'd been able to stay for a longer visit, but Archie is anxious to start our new life together."

"I want to say good-bye to Smokey. She's at Nana Philly's," I say. "You should see her before we go."

Mama takes a deep breath and looks down.

"My grandmother, I mean," I say.

"She said I wasn't her daughter anymore," Mama says. "She said I was a disgrace."

"Oh, Mama," I say. "I'm sure that's not the meanest thing she's ever said."

✳ ✳ ✳

Nana Philly looks just the same as when I first saw her: she's sitting in her chair wearing her long white nightgown, the silly red cloche hat on her head. Except now she's reading a new fashion magazine that I bought her and Smokey's sitting on her lap, content as can be.

"I've come to say good-bye," I say. "We're going to Georgia."

She looks up from the magazine.

"Maybe you can come visit sometime. I bet there's lots of kids you can be mean to there."

The corner of her mouth curls up.

"Take care of Smokey for me," I say, and hug her tiny body. She's just a bag of bones. "I'm gonna miss our lunches."

Her shaky hand smooths my hair.

"Me thoo," she says.

"There's someone else who wants to say good-bye," I say, and turn to the doorway. "Come in, Mama."

Mama steps into view.

Nana Philly looks startled.

"Mother," Mama says in a stiff voice.

Nobody moves for a moment.

Tears start falling from my grandmother's eyes,

and then Mama starts crying, too. The next thing I know, Mama's on her knees in front of Nana Philly and they're hugging each other like nothing ever happened.

A Hollywood writer couldn't have imagined a sappier scene.

I sit on the porch with Beans, Kermit, Buddy, and Ira. Mama's in the kitchen with Aunt Minnie and Uncle Vernon. Her happy laugh floats out the open window.

"Will you play marbles with me, Turtle?" Buddy asks.

"I don't have time, Buddy. We're leaving any minute."

"You think you'll come back and visit?" Kermit asks.

Beans smacks Kermit. "Don't give her any ideas. I just got my room back."

Pork Chop comes riding down the lane on his new bicycle.

"What are you doing here?" he asks me.

"I'm not gonna miss you, either," I say.

"No," he says, narrowing his eyes. "I mean, what are you doing here? I saw your new daddy leave."

"What?" I say.

"Dark hair? Panama hat? I saw him get on a boat hours ago. I figured you were with him."

The blood rushes in my ears, and I feel like I'm going to be sick.

Buddy inches away from me. "Are you gonna puke, Turtle?"

Archie's words ring in my head.

"Princess, everybody's got a dream."

And I know it's true. I've been had.

Archie sold me a dream — Mama happy, a home, a family at last — and I bought it hook, line, and sinker. Turns out I'm as much of a sucker as anybody.

"Do you know where the boat was headed?" Kermit asks Pork Chop, but he shakes his head.

"Easy enough to find out," Ira says.

I pull the five-dollar bill out of my pocket and stare at it. Then I crumple it.

"I need to know where he went," I say, and look in Beans's eyes. I was wrong. They're not the color of snot; they're the color of alligator pear.

Beans sets his cap low and nods grimly.

"Leave it to us," he says.

Mama and Aunt Minnie and Uncle Vernon are laughing over sweet tea in the kitchen when I walk in with the boys an hour later.

"Mama," I say.

She looks up at me, her eyes sparkling. "Archie outside?"

Now I know why those men jumped off roofs. They couldn't bear to see the light go out of a loved one's eyes—to know they'd let the person down.

"Archie's not coming, Mama."

"What?" she asks, still smiling.

I look across the table at Aunt Minnie. She knows at once what I'm saying.

"Oh, Sadiebelle," she murmurs.

"I don't understand?" Mama asks anxiously. "Did something happen to him?"

"He's gone, Mama," I say.

"Archie's dead?" Mama screeches.

"Well, Mami always says that Cuba is her idea of heaven," Pork Chop says.

"Cuba? What are you talking about?" she asks, bewildered.

Uncle Vernon sighs and looks down.

"Aunt Sadie! He took Turtle's part of the treasure and hopped a boat to Cuba!" Beans blurts out. "He's a no-good crook!"

Mama turns so pale I think she's going to faint.

"No," she whispers, staring past us like we're not even there.

"Please, Mama," I say, and I get that same feeling I get right before everything falls apart.

"I don't believe you!" she shouts at everyone, and then she's gone, running out the front door.

I leap up and chase after her. She's halfway down the lane when I catch up.

"Mama, stop!" I plead, grabbing her skirt. She whirls around, her face anguished, and collapses right in the middle of the muddy lane, tears running down her face.

"But he promised! He promised he'd take care of us!" she says, sobbing like she's dying. I feel her hurt like my own; it's the worst feeling ever. Uncle Vernon was right—I do have a soft underbelly.

It's Mama.

"Everything'll be fine," I tell her, but I'm lying.

There's never going to be a happy ending for us, and I feel a horrible pain in my chest and I know it's my heart, ripping open like a pair of Buddy's pants. And I can't help it; I start crying. I cry for everything—for poor Smokey getting burned up by those boys, for every mean word some kid said to me, for all the times one of Mama's fellas raised our hopes and dashed them. Most of all, I cry for my poor dumb heart for secretly believing that Mama and Archie and me could be a real family.

The tears rain down like spitballs, and there's no stopping them now. They're like a hurricane sweeping me away. Mama's drowning and she's dragging me under with her, and this time there's no one to rescue me. This time I'm not going to make it—

"Turtle!" Beans says.

I blink away tears to see him standing there with the rest of the boys, Aunt Minnie and Uncle Vernon behind them.

Beans elbows Pork Chop in the ribs.

"Uh, say, you want to be in the Diaper Gang?" Pork Chop asks me, looking uncomfortable.

"I don't like babies," I choke out.

"What about paper dolls?" Aunt Minnie asks, stepping forward. "I have some nice ones."

"But they're your dolls," I say.

"They belong to the family," my aunt says in a gruff voice. "So you're going to have to stay here if you want to play with them. Your mother, too."

I look back at the little Conch house. It will never be the Bellewood, with its modern attractive exterior and Venetian mirrored cabinet. But it doesn't seem quite so small or shabby to me anymore. I can see past the rickety porch and the tin roof and know it's built just like its people, to sway in a storm and not break.

"Aw, just say you'll stay, Turtle," Kermit says, and my heart swells like a sponge. Maybe the real treasure has been right here on Curry Lane the whole time—people who love Mama and me. A home.

Mama looks up. Her eyes are cloudy, but mine are clear.

"All right," I answer for us both. It may not be a Hollywood ending, but then I'm no Shirley Temple.

"Does that mean you'll play marbles with me now?" Buddy asks.

And then Beans makes a face at me. "Besides, you already got a dumb nickname like everyone else around here."

"Beans!" Aunt Minnie barks, but all I do is smile. I've lived long enough to learn the truth: not all kids are rotten, and there are grown-ups who are sweet as Necco Wafers.

And if you're lucky—*lucky as an orphan*—some of them may even end up being your family.

Author's Note

Turtle in Paradise was inspired by my Conch great-grandmother Jennie Lewin Peck, who emigrated with her family from the Bahamas to Key West in the late 1800s. As a child, I heard about Spanish limes and sugar apple ice cream and the importance of shaking out your shoes to avoid scorpions. My family is related to the Curry family of Key West, after whom Curry Lane is named.

Many families suffered hardship during the Great Depression, and it was not unusual for parents to leave home in search of work or for children to be cared for by relatives. Then, as now, entertainment was a great distraction, and movies, radio shows, and the funny pages provided much amusement for everyone. Little Orphan Annie, Shirley Temple, and the Shadow were all superstars in their day.

From the *Little Orphan Annie* comic strip, February 26, 1935

Shirley Temple popping through a 1935 calendar

At the height of the Depression, Key West was in economic ruin, with the majority of the population on public relief. The town officially declared bankruptcy. FERA, the Federal Emergency Relief Administration, came into Key West in 1934 with the intent of reinvigorating the economy by marketing it as a tourist attraction. Key West was on its way to recovery when what became known as the Labor Day Hurricane struck on September 2, 1935. While the Lower Keys and Key West were largely spared, the Middle and Upper Keys bore the brunt of the storm, with terrible loss of life.

Searching for pirate loot has always been a popular pastime in the Keys. Jeane Porter, in her book *Key West: Conch Smiles*, writes, "When I was a little girl in the early '30s everybody in Key West had a treasure story." While actually finding pirate treasure may seem far-fetched, historical rumors abound. In Charlotte Niedhauk's account of living in the Florida Keys during this time, *Charlotte's Story*, she relates the tale circulating around Key West of a sponge fisherman who mysteriously disappeared with his family to South America after finding the treasure of a pirate named Black Caesar. Whether Black Caesar ever visited the Keys is still a matter of speculation.

Pepe's Café is a beloved institution in Key West. It still exists, although it is no longer on Duval Street.

The sponging industry and turtle kraals are now

Pepe's Café, Key West, Florida, circa 1938

Key West children posing on the docks with five turtles and
a pile of sponges in the background

remnants of the past, but they were once thriving
industries. Nicknaming was a Key West tradition,
and the nicknames came in all styles. The scorpion
sting suffered by Aunt Minnie was inspired by an actual incident.

Likewise, some of the characters had their in-
spiration in actual people. The writer Ernest Hemingway was one of Key West's most famous residents.
He was in Key West when the Labor Day Hurricane

struck, and he witnessed the aftermath firsthand and wrote about it. In true Key West fashion, he had a nickname among the locals—Papa. Kermit was inspired by my cousin Kermit Lewin. The real Kermit suffered rheumatic fever as a child and grew up to become the mayor of Key West in the 1960s. He

The real Kermit (left) circa 1930, with the family friend who inspired Pork Chop

famously tricked Jimmy the ice cream man with the "nickel in the bottom of the cup" trick to get free ice cream, and he did tick-tock people. Killie the Horse and Jimmy were actual local characters of Key West.

Finally, the Diaper Gang's secret diaper-rash formula is a family remedy I have used on my own babies' bungys. (It also works on mosquito bites.)

My family's recollections, and those of many other Conchs, provided the details of everyday life in this book, and I am grateful to them all for sharing their memories.

A typical Conch neighborhood in Key West, circa 1935

Resources

Drye, Willie. *Storm of the Century: The Labor Day Hurricane of 1935*. Washington, D.C.: National Geographic Society, 2002.

Freedman, Russell. *Children of the Great Depression*. New York: Clarion Books, 2005.

Knowles, Thomas Neil. *Category 5: The 1935 Labor Day Hurricane*. Gainesville: University Press of Florida, 2009.

Terkel, Studs. *Hard Times: An Oral History of the Great Depression*. New York: The New Press, 2000.

Websites

Historical Preservation Society of the Upper Keys: keyshistory.org

Key West Art & Historical Society: kwahs.com

The Shadow's Sanctum: shadowsanctum.com

Acknowledgments

I would never have been able to write this book without the generosity of my Conch relatives, especially Cathy Porter, Kurt and Monica Lewin, and Ann Gardner. And, of course, my mother (who always shook out her shoes). I was fortunate to have incredible support from historian Annette Liggett; Tom Hambright, curator of the Florida History Department of the Monroe County May Hill Russell Library; and Jerry Wilkinson, president of the Historical Preservation Society of the Upper Keys. Willie Drye and Tom Knowles provided invaluable insight into the 1935 hurricane, and Anthony Tollin kindly aided my research on the Shadow. Harry Knight and Della Bennett were beyond generous in sharing their recollections of growing up in Key West in the 1930s, as was author and chronicler of all things Conch, Donnie Williams. Most of all, my heartfelt thanks to my editor, Shana Corey, who started me down this path by asking if my nana was really from Key West. She certainly was!

About the Author

JENNIFER L. HOLM'S great-grandmother emigrated from the Bahamas to Key West in 1897. Jennifer is the author of two other Newbery Honor Books, *Our Only May Amelia* and *Penny from Heaven*. She is also the author of several other highly praised books, including the Babymouse and Squish series, which she collaborates on with her brother Matthew Holm. Jennifer lives in California with her husband and two children. You can visit her website at jenniferholm.com.

Also from Jennifer L. Holm

A Newbery Honor Book

Turn the page for an excerpt!

When we get to the park, all the kids are gathered around the baseball diamond. Frankie's team is short of players, so Frankie has me be shortstop because of my arm. He says I can throw faster than any of the boys on the field.

By the second inning we're behind by one with two outs. Frankie's on first base, and another kid, Eugene Bird, is up at bat. Eugene looks nervous; he's not a very good hitter and he almost always strikes out. Not to mention he tried to kiss me once when we were in first grade.

Eugene swings and misses the pitch.

"Strike one!" the kid who's the umpire calls.

I'm sitting on the bench waiting for my turn at bat. Most of the girls don't play anymore; they sit on the side and watch. I'm thinking about Jack Teitelzweig and wondering if maybe I should be watching games instead of playing them when a girl with blond hair held back by a light-blue headband wearing a matching blue skirt makes her way over to where I'm sitting, trailed by two other girls. Just my luck.

"Having a nice summer, Penny?" Veronica Goodman asks with a fake smile.

I don't say anything. Mother says the only way

to deal with girls like Veronica is to ignore them, although Veronica is pretty hard to ignore.

"I hear you're working at the butcher shop," she says. "Sounds like a grand time!"

The girls titter. I do my best to ignore her, watching Eugene swing too late and miss the ball again.

"Strike two!"

Poor Eugene looks like he's going to faint from all the pressure. He knows Frankie will kill him if he strikes out again. Frankie hates to lose.

Veronica leans forward and says, "So tell me. Do you get to cut up pigs all day? How exciting! What about chickens? Do you get to cut up chickens, too?"

Veronica goes on and on and on. I don't know why, but something snaps, and it's as if I turn into another person, a person with no sense at all, because I hear myself saying, "Aw, shut up already."

"What did you say?" Veronica growls.

"Nothing," I mutter.

Over on first base, Frankie's straining toward me, trying to hear what we're saying.

"My father says we should have dropped the bomb on Italy. He said it would've gotten rid of all you traitors." Her voice rises a notch. "Who do you think you are, anyway? You and your dumb cousin think you're better than us?"

"At least I'm not mean," I say before I can stop myself. Maybe I *am* spending too much time around Frankie.

Her cheeks turn hot with anger. "Well, at least I don't have some crazy uncle who lives in a car and wears bedroom slippers all over town."

I go cold inside.

"Your uncle is off his rocker," she says, twirling a finger by her head. "Crazy as a loon."

That's it. It's one thing to pick on me, even on Frankie, but not Uncle Dominic.

"Don't talk about my uncle," I say, standing up.

"What are you gonna do about it, huh?" she asks with a smirk.

"This," I say, and I haul off and hit her hard across the face with my fist, just the way Frankie taught me.

Veronica squeals in pain. "My nose! My nose!"

"Penny!" Frankie shouts, and starts racing across the field.

Before he gets to me, Veronica smacks me hard, right in the eye, and I stagger back, and then

Frankie's leaping onto her, and the screaming begins and kids start pouring in and fists are flying and Eugene Bird doesn't have to worry if he's going to hit the ball after all, because that's the end of the game.

YEARLING!

Looking for more great books to read?
Check these out!

- ❏ *All-of-a-Kind Family* by Sydney Taylor
- ❏ *Are You There God? It's Me, Margaret* by Judy Blume
- ❏ *Blubber* by Judy Blume
- ❏ *The City of Ember* by Jeanne DuPrau
- ❏ *Crash* by Jerry Spinelli
- ❏ *The Girl Who Threw Butterflies* by Mick Cochrane
- ❏ *The Gypsy Game* by Zilpha Keatley Snyder
- ❏ *Heart of a Shepherd* by Rosanne Parry
- ❏ *The King of Mulberry Street* by Donna Jo Napoli
- ❏ *The Mailbox* by Audrey Shafer
- ❏ *Me, Mop, and the Moondance Kid* by Walter Dean Myers
- ❏ *My One Hundred Adventures* by Polly Horvath
- ❏ *The Penderwicks* by Jeanne Birdsall
- ❏ *Skellig* by David Almond
- ❏ *Soft Rain* by Cornelia Cornelissen
- ❏ *Stealing Freedom* by Elisa Carbone
- ❏ *Toys Go Out* by Emily Jenkins
- ❏ *A Traitor Among the Boys* by Phyllis Reynolds Naylor
- ❏ *Two Hot Dogs with Everything* by Paul Haven
- ❏ *When My Name Was Keoko* by Linda Sue Park